The Monster Upstairs

Elle Klass

The Monster Upstairs, Bloodseekers 2

Author's Disclaimer

Other Books by Elle

St. Augustine Novellas
Bloodseeker Series
The Vampires Next Door
The Monster Upstairs
The Ghost Within

hidden journals
Isandro vol. 1
Alarico vol. 2

Baby Girl Series
In the Beginning Book I
Moonlighting in Paris Book II
City by the Bay Book III
Bite the Big Apple Book IV
Caribbean Heat Book V
Return to the Bay VI
Prison of the Past VII
Baby Girl Box Set -Books I - IV

Zombie Girl
Premonition Book 1
Infection Book 2
Retribution Book 3

The Monster Upstairs, Bloodseekers 2

Prologue

The blitz of light blasted through the darkness and traveled over Mandy's bed, moving at the speed of light. Her blue eyes popped open and shifted towards the window. Climbing out of bed, she shuffled to the window and smoothed back the curtains. The light, now gone, left a feeling of unease nagging at her guts.

The air surrounding her suddenly grew muggy and dense trees and brush sprouted around her. Spinning in circles she couldn't see through the thick vegetation yet she knew she hadn't left her room. Confused more than scared, she reached out where her window had stood only seconds earlier. Now she felt damp air.

A faint sound like water rushing against the ground caught her attention, then the form of a woman. Her hair hung in long brown waves around her oval face. She wore a light blue slip dress. Her red lips mouthed something that Mandy couldn't determine, then the woman faded.

"Wait, don't go!" Mandy said as she lunged for the woman. Her face planting against the window as the muggy air and woods vanished.

Discombobulated, she stood for several seconds attempting to determine what had happened. Then a whisper in her ear said, *"St. Augustine."*

Mandy brought her hand to her ear then twisted her head. The room was void of life except for herself standing disoriented in a long purple T-shirt and sports underwear.

Who was St. Augustine and why do I need to know him or about him? What just happened? She stumbled backwards, falling atop her bed, and stared at the fan blades whirring above her head. Unable to sleep, she grabbed her phone from the white bedside dresser and yanked it off its charger. She plugged St. Augustine into the search engine and several links popped up; all indicating a city not a person.

She clicked on images and glanced through them. A coastal city in Florida. The oldest in the U.S. and surrounded by dense vegetation. *Was I there for a moment?*

She tossed her phone onto the bed beside her, her heart thumping steadily in her chest. The pictures played across her mind and a small voice echoed inside her head: *follow the light.*

Chapter 1

Two Days Later...

Mandy coasted her bicycle around the corner of her street. The large aspen tree marking her childhood home now in sight. Its broad shade and leaves always brought her comfort. She peddled up her driveway and toward the back fence and applied the brakes. Slipping off the seat of the bicycle, she opened the gate and walked the bike behind the fence, resting it against the house. This was her usual routine. As a star volleyball player she spent hours practicing after school, but today had been a meet so it was later than usual. Black clouds loomed in the evening sky, making it much darker than it should be, and the air was cool. Mandy shifted her blue eyes upwards and the first rain drop hit her face and ran down her cheek.

She enjoyed the steady rain falling on her as she walked toward the back door, a denim school bag hoisted over her right shoulder. Her heart stopped when she noticed the sliding glass door wide open. Her mother left it unlocked for her, but never open. The aroma of dinner hit her nostrils but turned her stomach as it smelled burned. She halted, her heart thumping inside her chest. Something was wrong, it was more than the door. A feeling crept into her guts and clung to her bones. Mandy wasn't the bravest of souls, but she wasn't a coward either. Sucking in a deep breath and scanning the yard and house she walked towards the open door.

A gust of wind blew from behind, pushing her dark hair over her face. She pulled off one of her many colorful wristbands and wrapped it around her shoulder length dark hair creating a messy ponytail with several chunks of her dark hair askew. Many thoughts fluttered through her brain as she moved closer to the back door. A few nights previous she'd awoken to large blasts of white light that lit up the sky like a fireworks display, only it wasn't a holiday, and then the whisper and voice in her head – *St. Augustine* and *follow the light* – she'd been uneasy since.

When she'd asked her mother, upstairs neighbor Joel, and friends, no one had noticed it but her. *How is that possible?* It was possible and she'd seen it. Mandy believed in the otherworldly and almost everything odd and supernatural. Her mother laughed it off saying, 'It was probably testing in the desert. You know they're always doing strange things out there.'

They didn't live in Area 51 and her mother's body language -- the shift in her eyes, tapping of her fingers, and tilt of her head -- told Mandy her mother wasn't being straight. No, there was something she knew but wasn't talking about. The feeling the light was meant for her hadn't left. She'd even had vivid dreams about bloodsucking beasts every night since. Their pointed fangs dripping crimson while their dark eyes called out to her, passing on a subliminal message: *you're ours*. Her body shuddered at the thought, yet she couldn't shake it. *Was it aliens? Were they at her house? Did they abduct her mother?*

She stood in front of the open doorway with one foot resting inside on the tile floor. Her eyes focused inside the room and her ears strained to listen. A faint choking sound forced her into action. Forgetting the aliens, bloodsuckers, and her fear, she dropped the denim bag off her shoulder and ran towards the sound. Careening around the corner to the kitchen, not watching where she was going, she slipped on the floor. As her body fell, her eyes widened as she saw her legs splayed before her in a scarlet puddle.

At first, confusion clouded her mind as it sorted through the red splotches across her pants. After a few seconds and more choking noises it clicked and her eyes shifted towards the weak sounds. Her mother lay only a few feet from her in a pool of blood, choking as she attempted to catch her breath.

"Mom!" she cried as she crawled across the floor toward her. Her mind completely focused on her mother, the idea of an intruder and possible danger didn't even register.

"Man… dy," she gurgled.

Mandy grabbed her mother's hand and wished with her entire soul for her to be whole. "What… what happened?"

"No t-i-m-e. Go… the drawer," she swallowed hard, "beneath our picture." More gurgling. "Ta-ke it out, turn… it… over," she spluttered with every ounce of her being and her eyes closed.

"Mom!" Mandy shook her gently and rested her head upon her mother's chest. Her tears fell in a heavy stream. "You can't die. You can't die," she chanted. Lifting her head, she placed her hands over her mother and concentrated. An overwhelming surge of power rushed through her body.

Her mother's eyes opened and her torso shot upright. "Mandy, do it now. Leave me!"

Mandy bolted skyward, flabbergasted at her mother's second wind then sobbed, "I can't. I love you."

A large hand touched Mandy's shoulder as her mother slumped back onto the floor and a deep voice she knew well said, "You have to, but not alone. I'll stay with you."

Mandy turned her head and looked at Joel. She hadn't heard him come into the house and he wasn't wet. It gave her a shock, then his warm brown eyes, filled with shards of gold, rested on hers. His dark hair combed back with the usual unruly lock above his left ear, otherwise not a hair out of place. He moved his hand from her shoulder and grasped her right hand. He lifted her up and, as if in an out of body experience, she walked with him to the drawer.

"Open it. Go ahead," he said, reassuring her as if her face belied her insecurity and confusion.

She choked back her sobs and peeked at her mother lying on the floor. Slowly she opened it. Pens, a stapler, a hole punch, phone book, and a small notepad – the one they used to message each other – lay inside it. She grabbed the notepad and stuffed it into her back pocket then flipped the drawer upside down.

There was an envelope labeled *Mandy* taped to the bottom. She peeled it off and held it to her chest.

"We need to go now," Joel said, his voice firm.

There was a part of Mandy, somewhere deep inside, that knew this day would happen. And the unusual display of lights a few nights previous was a call for her. Not only was it odd but it stirred something inside her. Sniffling, she rushed towards her mother who was now lying still, her hazel eyes glazed. They looked like fall grass, mostly green with specks of brown. "I love you," she whispered as she kissed her mother for the last time.

Lifting her head, she glanced at her mother's face – her left cheek against the floor -- and spotted something she hadn't seen earlier – two puncture holes in her carotid artery.

Chapter 2

Joel took Mandy's vacant hand as she stuffed the envelope into the front pocket of her jeans. "It's time."

"The police, someone murdered my…" her voice drifted off and tears exploded from her eyes as Joel dragged her towards the door.

He said nothing as he grabbed the knob and twisted. Mandy bumped into his back when he froze in the doorway. She felt his heart beating quickly inside his chest and his body radiated heat. She took a step back and looked on the other side of the door. A pair of khaki slacks and dark brown shoes were moving towards them. Something was wrong, very wrong.

"There's no time. They're here," he said in an unusually husky voice, slamming the door.

As the words left his mouth, cracking sounds ricocheted in the house. She peered through the room but saw nothing until she planted her eyes on Joel. His body distorted as claws formed where his nails had previously been. His appendages grew brown fur with silver tips and each bone in his spine cracked in his back as he dropped to all fours. A ripped pile of his clothes lay beneath him.

Awe-stricken, Mandy watched his transformation that took only seconds. Her jaw dropped as he turned to face her. His snout moved as his mouth opened.

"Get on my back!"

Mandy stared at him, blinking, unable to believe what she'd witnessed.

"Now Mandy, we have to go!"

It sounded like Joel, but the words dropped from the mouth of an animal. His fur was dark brown with silver on his underbelly and tips. Words shouldn't be coming from an animal's mouth and not in Joel's voice. It was a surreal moment and glimpse of her life to come. The synapses in her brain snapped into place and imminent danger and her dead mother became a reality. The talking wolf, however, was still surreal. "How the… you're a…"

"Wolf," he said, finishing her words. "We don't have time. I'll explain later." He nudged her belly hard with his snout, enough that she dropped on top of him as something heavy hit the front door. It sounded like the man in the khakis was hitting it with a battering ram. The walls of the house shook and pictures dropped off the walls.

Mandy's head hit his rump and she grabbed him around the middle with her legs flailing to the side. She struggled to bring them to his sides as he ran through the house, her head buried in fur. He stopped short of the back door and growled. Mandy lifted her head and turned to the side. In front of him was the large man with sharp teeth dressed in khaki pants. He looked like one of the bloodsucking monsters from her dreams.

Joel crushed his jaws together as he bit at the man, getting a firm grasp of his slacks as he ripped them, exposing the man's leg and a gaping bite wound from Joel's sharp teeth.

"You gnarly beast, give me the girl!" the large man demanded.

Mandy folded her fingers together and held on tight. She wasn't allowing the man in the khakis, probably the same one who killed her mother, to get hold of her.

Joel took a few steps backward into the house and the man placed his foot over the threshold. Joel growled, backed up, and got a running start as he leapt through the living room window.

Mandy howled and tucked her head as the majority of the glass broke, shards dropping over her back and crashing to the ground. At that moment, she was glad she rode him backwards. He jumped and dodged obstacles she couldn't see as she squeezed her eyes shut and buried her face in his fur and kept it there, her arms tucked tightly around his mid-section.

Loud blasts echoed through her ears. Her own curiosity forced her to look up. What she saw made her eyes widen. A group of several men and women surrounded her house. Her eyes enlarged more as a small tornado swirled towards the living room of her home. It moved from the fingertips of a young woman, developing and growing in a black cloud as it left her hands.

Mandy's eyes fixed on the woman. Her dark hair blowing behind her as the wind from the tornado pushed it and her backwards. She held her ground as the funnel cloud grew larger. Suddenly, a blast of white light caught the woman and she blew apart from the inside out as if she was made of porcelain and a bomb had blown up inside her. Mandy gasped, watching the scene in disbelief.

She'd never doubted the supernatural existed, but hadn't witnessed it first hand, and certainly didn't understand how she and her mother fit into the craziness. They lived a really normal existence in suburban Flagstaff, Arizona. Her mother worked as a crossing guard and Mandy did everyday teenage stuff; star volleyball player, mostly As and Bs in school except the AP Literature class she'd decided to take where she was struggling just to make a C. But nothing out the usual. She was an average teen whose main stress in life was passing the driving test in two weeks so she could get her license.

Joel's speed picked up and her home soon became a barely visible dot through the trees. The ground beneath them swished by so fast it became a blur of green and brown. She buried her face in his fur. Sets of other footsteps ran in sync with Joel's, but she didn't lift her head to see what they were.

Chapter 3

Joel's pace slowed and he jogged to a stop. "It's safe to get off now," he said, his breath even. She expected him to be breathless after his marathon run with her on his back, but he wasn't. It puzzled her, but no more than anything else that had happened in the past hour or so.

Adrenaline from the near-death experience rushed through her veins. She lifted her head and chest. Two other wolves sat on their haunches behind him. She uncurled her fingers clinging to his body and lifted herself up, then reluctantly got off his back. They were surrounded by several other wolves. One carried a duffle bag in its mouth.

Once she'd stood, Joel changed back into a man. His snout shrunk, all his body fur curled back into his body, and only the dark, jumbled waves and kinky curl was left on his head. His claws shortened into fingernails as his paws became hands and feet.

Her eyes grew as she watched, unable to synthesize what was happening and seeing him naked in front of her. She'd had boyfriends, but nothing serious. She gulped, eying his beautiful, muscled body, then turned her head as she felt her cheeks redden. *He's gorgeous,* she thought. *How have I never noticed before?* Because she'd never seen him in the nude before.

The Duffle Bag Wolf dropped the bag at Joel's feet and he opened it, pulling out a pair of jeans that fit snug around his cute round butt and pulled a blue T-shirt over his head.

"We'll stay here for the night," said a gorgeous female white wolf. There wasn't a touch of any other color on her body. She looked like snow.

Joel nodded. "We'll complete the journey tomorrow at daybreak," he confirmed as if he was in charge.

All the wolves nodded in unison, like they had an unspoken language and passed words through their minds instead of their mouths. With everything she'd seen in the past couple hours she didn't doubt it and chuckled out loud as she thought it. Every wolf eye shifted towards her. She stopped giggling and followed up with a crooked smile but said nothing.

Joel picked up the bag and took Mandy's hand as they headed across the street to a motel. It wasn't anything special, a couple long, one-story buildings with white stucco. A few large flowering cacti that sat in dark orange planters on either side of the front door and a small water garden with a frog spouting a drizzle of water from his mouth was on the other side of the large U driveway.

Mandy stayed silent, lost in her thoughts. It all made sense even though it made no sense. Her dream wasn't a dream at all, but a vision of sorts. The light, blasted through the night, was her call to action. *But what was happening?* She was a normal sixteen-year-old girl, who believed in the strange and the weird and now it found her in spades.

Joel paid for the room and they gave him a plastic keycard. They pushed through the glass door and it jingled as they walked outside into the chilly, dry desert air and followed the sidewalk. A large greenish pool with a dirty white fence surrounding it and a few tattered loungers separated the buildings.

Inside, the tiny room wasn't an improvement, she noted, scanning her surroundings. It had one full-size bed decorated with a blue and black checked bedspread. The curtain hanging over the only window in the room matched. A plush chair with a couple small holes stood in front of the window at an angle, with a small wooden table between it and a wooden chair. The air smelled heavily of vanilla air freshener.

She staggered to the bed and sat, expecting it to be saggy. Instead, it was firm and solid. In a partial lucent daze she asked, "What just happened?"

He sighed. "We knew this day might happen."

She echoed his sigh. Should she yell at him, cry, or fess up to all the emotions and strange thoughts in her head. Joel saved her, he'd been a part of her life as long as she could remember, so she fessed up and pushed any angry thoughts deep inside her. "What's weird is so have I. I can't explain it, but I've always felt like half of a whole and since my vision I've felt a strong pull to do something, but I don't know what." She paused. Anger rose inside her as she realized both Joel and her mother knew something and lied to her.

She pushed it down again. "My vision. You knew when I told you. Why weren't you straight with me?"

His eyes shot to the ground. "It wasn't time."

"Time! Time for what?!" No longer hiding her anger. She knew she was displacing it and didn't have a clue what was happening but she wanted answers and the chance to vent the fury rising inside her.

He shifted on his feet. "There's... it's complicated."

The air between them silent as Mandy seethed and Joel stood stock still, his hands in his pockets.

"And you, you're, you're... a werewolf," she spat out, then calmed. A beautiful werewolf who just saved her life. It didn't so much surprise her as she needed processing time and answers.

"You have the envelope?" he asked, ignoring her outburst.

He always had a way of defusing her wrath. She admitted it was probably because he was downright gorgeous and sensible, always sensible and after today she had a new appreciation for Joel as a man, not Joel her neighbor.

"What?" She furrowed her brows, momentarily confused.

"From your mother."

She nodded then dug the wrinkled envelope out of her pants. Straightening it out, she peeled back the sealed flap. Inside was a letter. She read it out loud.

"Honey,

These aren't the words I ever wanted to tell you, but I always knew it was your destiny. You are possibly the single most important person on this planet and it was mine and Joel's job to keep you safe. Your life is about to change drastically and you'll question everything you ever knew. Promise me you will stay by Joel's side.

Love Mom"

Mandy blinked several times as she stared t the letter in her hand, tears welling in the corners of her eyes as she absorbed her mother's words. "What is she talking about, Joel?" she asked, her eyes staring blankly at the floor while her anger subsided and sadness filled its place. She fought back her tears.

"Everything she said is true."

She'd known Joel for as long as she could remember and he'd always lived in the apartment above them. The house had a downstairs and an upstairs but were two separate homes, like a duplex. She turned her eyes toward Joel and peered at him beneath her messy bangs, several chunks of hair sticking up and out of her messy ponytail.

He reached out and grabbed her hands, giving them a squeeze. With an attempted smile she squeezed back, but her body was weak from the overwhelming sadness and emptiness she felt knowing her mother was gone.

"Joel."

"Yeah, Man," he answered in his deep yet gentle voice.

He always called her *Man* instead of Mandy. She considered her words before speaking. He was the closest thing she had to a sibling, yet something was amiss. "How did you know?"

"About your mother?" he asked in a timid voice. The one he used when playing stupid like when he wouldn't tell her where her mother hid the Christmas presents.

"Yeah, how did you know?"

He licked his lips, his hand still firmly grasping hers. "I didn't, not exactly. It was more a gut feeling."

She forced her head back and blew out a breath of air. She was tired and mentally exhausted, yet curious about their excursion, her mother's strange letter, and what the heck Joel was talking about. "Don't be cryptic, please give me a straight answer. What is all this about?"

He blinked, then released a breath as he let go of her hands and sat on the bed next to her. "I'm a werewolf and we protect each other. Normally, we don't get involved in business that isn't ours, unless," he paused for a second, "it relates to protecting one of ours."

Mandy stared at him, her eyes cold. She didn't want riddles but answers and she wasn't a werewolf -- at least, she didn't think so.

He shifted his eyes from her cold stare. "Your mother wasn't really your mother, she's mine. Our jobs were to protect you. Your parents showed up on hallowed werewolf grounds. My mother, Selenia, found them and allowed them in, with permission of course. I don't know everything, she would never tell me, but I do know your parents were witches and your birth was something special, something the werewolves felt an obligation to protect at all costs. You are the one is all Selenia told me. Afterwards, we knew they'd come for you eventually and so we hid you in Arizona."

Overwhelmed, she wrapped her hands over her cheeks. "Exactly what are you saying?"

"You inherited a gift. I'm not sure what that gift is, only that the wolves consider you the savior of humanity and protecting you is essential. Carlito will explain the rest."

She pondered for a minute, the silence between them quiet enough to hear the gears in her head shifting. "My mother who raised me is my mother. No one else! And what happened to the woman who birthed me and the man who planted the seed inside her?"

"She couldn't raise you. Your life would have been in grave danger, and her powers were not strong enough to fight the world. But the powers you inherit can bring peace and healing to the world. Your father is well... another story."

He heaved then continued, Mandy's eyes drilling a hole into his head. He had no choice. "Your mother is a witch of the light. Your father a witch of the night -- a dark witch. They fell in love -- forbidden love -- and when she learned she was pregnant they ran to save your life. If they knew you existed they'd have battled for you, You are the light."

Mandy blurted, "They found me! That's what all this is about, but how? How Joel?"

His brown eyes dropped, "I don't know," he paused for several seconds then continued the story. "With nowhere to run, your parents' came to us on the chance you were the next to bear the power and it so happened you are."

Mandy's stare didn't budge while her mind attempted to process everything Joel told her. *I'm some princess of the light? A witch of sorts. Ha!* The darn light and strange vision was beginning to make sense. On a normal day in her humdrum life she would have told him he was insane, but not today. What power was he talking about and light and dark? Geez, it sounded like an episode of Star Wars. *Was she like Princess Leia and, if so, where was Luke?*

She let out a deep sigh and fell backwards on the bed, cupping her hands over her eyes and mumbled, "If I'm some kind of witch where are my powers?" Then she remembered the tornado woman and the light that blew her apart and she spoke before Joel could answer her last question. "Am I like the people who destroyed my house? Were they witches?"

The bed shook slightly as Joel stood. He ran his hands down his jeans, ignoring her questions. "Are you hungry?"

Mandy didn't respond right away. Food was the last thing on her mind, but her stomach protested against her mind at the mention of the word. "I'll try," she responded.

He nodded, although she didn't see it as her hands were still planted over her eyes.

"I saw a burger place across the street," he said, then slipped the room key in his back pocket. "Don't leave, the wolves have a close eye on this place. You're safe here."

She hadn't considered leaving -- or even moving. Her body felt dead inside. At the moment she didn't even care if she was a supernatural princess or witch of some kind.

Once he was gone, the deafening silence in the room drove her mad. Her mind replayed the events starting with finding her mother near death on the kitchen floor with bite marks in her neck. "Bite marks?" she questioned the air.

With that thought, she squeezed her eyes shut and focused on her mom's neck. Yes, they were bite marks but from whom? *OMG! The man in the khakis, like the creatures in my dreams. Not only are werewolves real but so are... vampires...*

Frustrated, tired, confused, worried, and with a jumble of knots in her stomach, she got up slowly and zombie-shuffled into the bathroom. She filled the tub with warm water then searched for something to make bubbles. All she found was shampoo so she dumped it into the water. Once it was full she shut the water off and peeled her nasty clothes from her body. Her jeans dropped in a puddle onto the linoleum floor. Dried blood covered her entire butt and thighs. She sniffled, remembering how it got there, then sank into the warm water, allowing it to carry her away. Mandy untwisted the wristband in her hair and ducked her head beneath the surface of the water then lifted it and pushed the water out of her eyes and blinked.

Within a few minutes her eyes fluttered and closed. Behind her lids she felt herself clinging to Joel. His wolf form strong and his fur soft. His naked body came into view, his strong chest and chiseled muscles that exploded all over his body. For the first time, she let her thoughts explore him and didn't fight her growing attraction to him.

Her mind wandered to Keller, a boy she'd dated for a while. It was the most serious relationship she'd had and she'd felt giddy inside every time he took her hand or gave her a kiss, until she discovered he had another girlfriend at another school.

It was by accident she found out. The day after school let out in June. The air outside was hot and dry, but the mall was cool and air conditioned. She'd been applying for jobs, hoping to make a little money over the summer when she saw Keller's unmistakable dark hair with the blond chunk on top pulled back into a ponytail. He stood outside the arcade. She walked towards him but, as she got closer, realized he wasn't hanging out with his friends or talking on the phone but with another girl.

He grabbed her hand then snaked his other around her middle and dropped a kiss -- not a friendly peck but a long, drawn out tongue kiss. The same kind he gave her. Tears in her eyes, she ran out of the mall and called Joel to pick her up.

A drive that normally took Joel fifteen minutes took him nearly forty that day. While she waited, sweating in the dry air that grew drier, hotter and more miserable, but knowing she couldn't go back inside with the chance of seeing him again, Keller called. His voice strained, he fessed up and apologized. How he knew she'd seen anything was a surprise to her. As she strolled down memory lane she remembered Joel had a satisfied smirk on his face as he pulled the car up. She'd never forget it. A smile parted her lips as she understood now that Joel had taken care of Keller for her. Scared the bejesus out of him. She wondered if he'd displayed any of his werewolf or just brute strength.

Clearly he'd done something. His kind yet protective personality. His eyes and the perfect curve of his chin. *Stop it!* she ordered herself. It's Joel, the boy you've known all your life. Then it hit her. He always lived above them and hadn't ever really aged.

"Is that possible?" she asked out loud. She'd never considered it before. When she was little she'd thought him a teen, when she grew older she considered him a young man. *How old is he really?*

Her thoughts of Joel brought on feelings of guilt. So concerned with herself and the loss of her mother she hadn't given one lick for Joel. She was his biological mother, not hers. Her whole life she hadn't known that. A secret they'd kept from her. It dawned on her now and she shrunk downward in the tub feeling her own shame and embarrassment for not acknowledging it when Joel told her and for only thinking about herself, especially when Joel always put her first. *How could I be so selfish and inconsiderate?*

The motel door creaked open, knocking her thoughts into oblivion and reminding her of the current danger. A shiver ran over her spine and she sat very still. *What if it isn't Joel?*

Chapter 4

Her heart thumped like a drunken drummer inside her chest as she attempted to calm her breathing. She glanced around the room for a weapon. If she had super powers she didn't know what they were or have any idea how to use them. Nothing. It was a cheap motel bathroom -- was she going to attack the intruder with a towel?

Footsteps pounded against the floor, muffled by the carpeting, then a knock sounded on the door.

She sighed. Someone wanting to hurt her wouldn't knock and ask permission. Death by towel would have to wait.

"Man, you in there?"

Joel's voice sailed through the air and calmed the rest of her body, her breathing and heart rate returned to normal. "Getting out now." Feelings of guilt clouded her mind as she slipped her clothes back on, except her pants. She couldn't wear them again covered in her mother's blood. Another wave of tears poured down her cheeks and she sat on the toilet sobbing.

The door opened a sliver. "Man?"

When she didn't respond he opened the door and rushed to her, folding his arms around her neck and drawing her close. A large dose of his scent wafted through her nostrils, even through her stuffy nose she smelled him. A slight musk with a touch of sweetness. *Damnit, stop thinking about him like that!* He lowered his chin, resting it on top of her head. She felt his body shudder against her.

"Joel," she said through sobs.

He pushed her closer to him and she realized he was crying too. She was his mother too. She should be comforting him not the other way around. "I'm sorry." She nuzzled her ear against his hard abs and pulled her arms tightly around him. She wanted him to feel how sorry she was and understand her sorrow wasn't only for herself but his loss too. She didn't dare speak though, as a man crying was a sight seldom seen and she didn't want to disturb the moment.

After several minutes, he let go and moved a couple steps backwards. His eyes still reddened from crying. "I got us food, we need it and rest before our journey tomorrow." He turned on his heel and walked out the door.

She collected herself and walked into the other room, he turned his head towards her and his eyes doubled as they took in her body stopping at her bare legs just below her girl briefs.

Her cheeks reddened in sync with his. "I couldn't put those pants back on."

His gaze shifted away from her and he lifted a large cup with a straw to his mouth. She joined him at the small table. Without a word he lifted a huge burger out of a Styrofoam container and took a bite. He'd always liked rare meat, just like her mother, and now she recognized why – wolves like fresh meat.

Mandy, on the other hand, liked medium well, only the tiniest bit of red in the center. Sitting at the small wooden table across from him, she took a second container as he slid it her way. If tomorrow was going to be anything like today she needed to eat. Maybe tomorrow she'd get on his back and rest her head above his and enjoy the softness of his fur. A day ago she'd have considered the thought ludicrous but today, at the moment, it was wonderful.

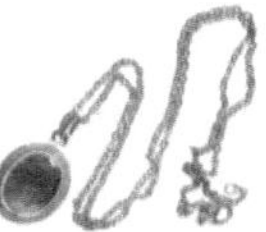

"I'll take the chair," Joel offered.

Mandy glanced at it. The bed was firm and the chair looked as though it had been stolen from a junk yard. "No you won't. You need rest since you're the one doing all the running. The bed is large enough for both of us." She pointed at her girl briefs. "I have my big girl panties on tonight."

He smiled and raked a hand through his hair, pulling his unruly curl out but it bounced back when he let the hair go. She loved his smile, realizing it was the first time she'd seen it since yesterday.

Mandy curled to one edge of the bed and he curled to the other. The air conditioner on full blast, she curled the covers under her chin to stay warm. There was no fight for the covers though, as he slept without them. He'd always run hot and she pondered *is it a werewolf thing?*

She awoke in the night after several strange dreams. Feeling Joel next to her, she remembered they weren't dreams but her life. Joel turned and flopped an arm around her. Instead of moving it she wrapped it around her and buried her face in his chest, falling back to sleep listening to his heartbeat.

She awoke to the sound of pouring water. In her half-awake daze she thought it was raining, then saw Joel walk out of the bathroom with only his jeans on. The water was merely the shower. She sighed and admired Joel's physique. He was all she had now.

"Are you ready?" he asked, in a far perkier tone than she felt.

"What time is it?" she asked, wiping the sleep out of her eyes.

"Sunrise."

She remembered his words to the other wolves, 'We leave tomorrow at daybreak and nodded as she climbed out of bed. The clothes on her body were wrinkled. She hoped wherever they were going that they'd have clean clothes for her. Now wasn't the time to worry about it, or her hair, which she knew was standing at various angles as it did every morning.

She staggered to the bathroom and on the counter lay a hairbrush and a toothbrush along with a tube of toothpaste and a pair of grey sweats. Her lips curled into a smile and she ran the brush through her unruly hair and scrubbed her nasty hamburger-morning breath teeth, finally pulling the sweats on. They weren't a perfect fit, and sagged a bit in the butt, however, they would do. She grabbed her wristband off the side of the tub and wrapped her bundle of thick hair in it. *It'll have to do*, she thought as she shifted a chunk of hair that stuck out like a turkey feather.

After she peed, she glanced in the mirror one last time then strolled into the bedroom and slipped her shoes on. "I'm ready."

"That's it?"

She raised an eyebrow. "We need to leave right?"

He nodded. "We do. The more time we have on the road the better the chance we get there tonight."

They stole across the street, the sun hovering over the horizon shading the sky in pinks, golds and a light shade of violet. She shivered from the cool air and wrapped her arms around her chest. Joel carried the duffle bag which contained the hairbrush, their toothbrushes and toothpaste and her bloodied pants. She couldn't see the other wolves until they made it into the woods and they came out of their hiding places, surrounding them.

Within minutes they were on the road again. The trees rushing past her. She had no idea where they were or where they were going except it was a place where everything would be revealed to her by some man named Carlito.

Power, good, evil, whatever her destiny, it was all waiting at the end of her journey and she didn't think any of it would surprise her. *Hah!* She rolled her eyes as she buried her chin into the top of Joel's head and let his fur tickle it. She was content for the moment to snuggle as tight to him as she could. It kept her body warm against the chilly fall air and it felt good.

With nothing but time she remembered her vision and cryptic woman and creeping feeling, along with the spooky voice *Follow the light, St. Augustine.* The light was her destiny, she felt it, but *what was the light? Where were they going? How did so many people know secrets about her and she had no clue?* She closed her eyes and allowed the vision to take her back.

Mandy nuzzled his ear and whispered, "Are we going to St. Augustine?" His pace faltered for a second and she thought maybe he was going to stop, but then his pace picked up. He didn't respond.

As the day wore on, the woods became denser and the air moist, like her dream. For hours she'd been lost inside her own mind. It was a kaleidoscope of thoughts until something crashed hard to the ground beside her. She nearly lost her balance and fell off Joel's back but she was able to catch her fall by wrapping her legs around him and grabbing the stack of wristbands covering her arm. She shifted her weight and laid her chest flat against his back, making herself more aerodynamic.

Joel swiftly dodged the falling tree. Mandy peeked over his fur and watched the mammoth tree fall to the ground, taking a couple smaller ones with it. More trees crashed, the sound echoing through the woods. Mandy ducked and clutched Joel tight around his middle. She guessed the storm wasn't natural but supernatural, like the tornado that took out her home and the shattering witch.

The bright sun disappeared in an instant and heavy rain and pellets of hail dropped from the sky, beating against Mandy's back. Joel continued his pace and the other wolves branched off to the sides. Trees dropped as Joel jumped over and slid under them with ease. Mandy hung on for her life. She buried her face into the back of his neck. His pace slowed and finally stopped.

A damp, mildewy smell rose into her nostrils and she lifted her head. They were surrounded by darkness.

"Stay quiet," Joel urged in a whisper.

Judging by the smell and the darkness they were underground, a cave or man-made structure of some kind. She wasn't exactly sure and resisted the urge to ask where they were.

He sat on his haunches and she slid off his back and sat cross-legged on the cold ground. She scooted on her rump around him and leaned towards where she thought his ear should be. She made out its faint outline through the darkness. It was upright and in listening mode so she whispered, "What's happening?"

"They found us. The others split off to find and dispose of our attackers."

That confirmed her suspicions but what did he mean dispose of their attackers? That didn't sound good, but she didn't ask what he meant. Mandy blinked her eyes as they slowly adjusted to the darkness and she saw the outline of his wolf form in front of her. He shifted, and nudged his snout against her. It was wet, yet sent tingles through her body.

After a couple minutes she figured it was as good a time as any to ask him her question once again. "Are we going to St. Augustine?"

He wiggled his snout and shook it in a no. "I'm taking you to my home... to see Carlito," he said, his voice barely audible.

She twisted her lips and let out a sigh.

"I'm going to check the entrance, stay here and stay quiet," he demanded, not entertaining St. Augustine.

She sat still and watched his shadow form move on. The eerie quiet spooked her and she heard steps, it sounded like an animal of some sort. She scooted against the cave wall, hoping the steps belonged to Joel or that her silly mind was playing tricks on her. She pushed her ear against the wall to feel vibrations. Something was definitely moving inside the cave. The vibrations seemed to come from two directions.

She curled her legs to her chest and wound her arms around them, clasping her hands together. In a few minutes she heard sniffing and smelled wet fur but couldn't make out the form. It hadn't yet entered the groove of cave she sat in.

Something tickled against her neck and she reached a hand to bat it away, thinking it was a nasty spider. When she touched it, the critter whipped around her neck and dragged her upwards. She opened her mouth to scream but something firm and pointed climbed into her mouth and lashed against the inside of her cheek. She gagged and spat, weaving her head to the side. It moved, brushing against her face below her left eye, and tightened its grip around her neck. Her hands dropped to her sides as her legs stretched out. She bucked against it and grasped her hands around its smooth skin trying to loosen it before it choked her.

Mandy gasped for breath as it continued dragging her upward against the cave wall. She felt her body lift from the ground, her feet unable to touch anything but empty air. It coiled tighter around her and she let out a choked, "Jo...el." She felt her air supply shorten as she wheezed. The more she inhaled and fought the creature the more difficult it was for her to breathe. She stopped fighting it and gathered her strength to call once more for Joel but she only squeaked, "Jjj."

Heavy steps pounded against the cave floor and a large creature rose in front of her, extending its bulky claw and swiping against her neck, barely missing her face. She dropped to the ground and something heavy dropped with her and hit the cave floor with loud thuds on both sides of her.

"Are you OK?" asked a female voice. She recognized it as the beautiful white wolf.

"Yes. I think so," Mandy replied, rubbing her neck and puffing for breath.

"I'm Calypso but everyone calls me Caly," she said as more footsteps entered the dark part of the cave. Immediately she recognized the musky scent as Joel.

"What was that thing?" she asked Calypso.

"You don't want to know," she responded in a dread-filled tone.

"Where are the others?" asked Joel.

"Others?" Mandy asked.

Caly spoke at the same time, "They'll catch up when they're finished."

"Let's move," responded Joel, ignoring Mandy's question.

Instead of feeling perturbed and upset over being ignored, she sighed with relief as she'd rather face whatever was outside. At least she could see what was coming rather than take the chance another something would attack her in the dark.

"I came in the back, follow me," Caly said, sniffing the air.

They padded through a series of tunnels, Caly in the lead, Joel in the rear, and Mandy in the middle. A small glimmer of light brightened as they neared the exit. Relief washed over Mandy.

Within a couple minutes they exited the cave. Mandy squinted her eyes from the bright sun. A violet haze hung high in the atmosphere. It was an unreal sky, as if they'd entered the cave on earth and exited in another realm. Strangely, she felt comforted by the violet glow.

"If we head straight east we'll make it in less than an hour, but it's a more populated area," Caly said.

Joel responded, "We need to get her there as quick as possible. They'll be back."

Mandy huffed, "What the heck? Who is after me? I don't even have powers. I'm a teenager who wants a shower and a clean change of clothes. Is it possible everyone has me confused with someone else?" She knew better. A part of her had always known, but her life was in chaos, her mother gone forever and she had to get her licks in. She considered leaving them and going on her own, then glanced at Joel's dark eyes, gold flecks radiating bright and knew she had to stick with him.

Joel met her gaze. "No, you are the one. It's the dark witches. They have the power to wield Earth's elements and every minute we stand here talking we run the risk they'll find us again before we make it there."

Mandy nodded. It made sense and explained the magic she'd witnessed around her home. It was the witches who destroyed it and were bent on finding her now. *But didn't Joel say her biological parents were witches?* She was ready for answers.

"You ride with Calypso. She is the fastest and can get you there the quickest," ordered Joel.

"Climb on," she said, moving closer to Mandy.

Mandy shrugged and hoisted herself onto Caly's back. She wasn't as thick around as Joel but her muscles were every bit as firm and her fur soft as a silken pillow.

"Hold on. He wasn't kidding. We'll get there in half the time."

The second Mandy was onboard securely, Caly took off. The trees rushed past them so quick they appeared as a green blur. She tucked her head into Caly's neck to protect her face against the rush of wind. She smelled of wet dog with a slight aroma of jasmine.

Chapter 5

Alison and the Slayers

Alison curled her lips as she mindlessly scribbled down notes. Veronica hadn't been back to school since she was kidnapped by the night witch and they were no closer to tracking down Rodham and Adrian's amulets. Veronica, their fairweather witch, night or light they didn't know, but she liked to think she was good even though her personality lacked a positive side.

It all happened only a few nights ago yet felt like a lifetime. Less than a couple months ago she was the new girl and had a harmless crush on the boy next door, until their strange neighbors moved in and she and Rodham teamed up, breaking into their apartment and finding Rodham's emerald amulet and the slayer journal. From that point life got crazy and even crazier when her Gran visited and she learned she was the next in line to bear the garnet amulet with the power of invisibility. Gran bore the amulet for centuries and now it was her turn.

She also missed mind talking with Rodham. As the current emerald Slayer he had the ability to read minds and telecommunicate. Since his amulet was seized by the night witch with silver hair who stole Veronica his powers were gone. He flashed a smile at her. She flashed one back. The good part was they could kiss and hold hands without a blast of electricity sizzling their insides.

Along with accepting the amulet and its responsibility she had to accept that she and Rodham couldn't be together. As Slayers, the electricity between them was too powerful for them to continue as boyfriend and girlfriend, unless they wanted to fry their guts. Holding hands was the most they could do and only for short moments or to channel their powers. She sighed. It was a catch 22, either he had his amulet and powers and they could communicate telepathically and save the world from Bloodseekers, or he didn't have it and they could make out.

The day after the incident, she and Lacey went to Veronica's house. An older man with wrinkly skin and a saggy neck opened the door. According to him, no Veronica lived there. What surprised her more than his lie -- or Veronica's, she didn't yet know -- was the youthfulness in his voice. It belied his age.

With no other option, they left. His eyes stayed on them from the window until they were out of his sight. Both Alison and Lacey were so freaked out they practically ran back to Alison's. She'd wished then that Rodham had his amulet because there was something seriously disturbing about the whole situation but neither she nor Lacey had the ability to dig around inside his mind and she was back to her dilemma; Rodham having his amulet and powers, or his soft, full lips pressed against hers. A small pang of guilt pinged at her insides as she thought about it.

The bell rang and her thoughts returned to the present. She closed her notebook and shoved it inside her backpack then hoisted it over her shoulder. Rodham grabbed her hand and she laced her fingers through his as they walked to his car.

"You're quiet. What's up?" asked Rodham.

"I don't know. I have a creepy feeling in my guts that I can't shake and I can't stop thinking about everything."

He nodded and unwrapped his hand from hers, draping his arm around her shoulder.

"It's like something's coming, something big. I can almost feel its pulse inside me."

"I feel it too, but I think it's from the weirdness the other night. I haven't seen any sight of Bloodseekers or witches. Have you?"

"No," she said in a soft voice. "I think we took care of the Bloodseeker problem for a while." She knew, eventually, they'd face them again.

They approached his car and she tossed her bag into the backseat of his Charger and scooted onto the front passenger seat. They rode home in silence. Alison's mind drifted and her Gran's face floated across it. She and her mom put Gran on a plane the day after they blitzed the Bloodseeker village into oblivion.

She worried every day and Skyped her yesterday. The wrinkles in her skin webbing across what was once a perpetually youthful face. She now looked like a grandmother but maintained her energetic personality. She cringed, knowing age would continue creeping up on her until her true age showed, then she'd pass. It was the curse of passing the garnet amulet to Alison. She pushed the thought away; she didn't want to think about it.

Rodham pulled into a parking space outside their apartment building. "Things are going to work out. We'll find Veronica and the amulets."

She sighed. "I don't know where to start looking. I've read my journal cover to cover so many times I've memorized it. There's no clues inside it."

He leaned over the console and kissed her cheek. The touch of his soft lips against her flesh excited her libido and she turned her head. Their lips met in a drawn out full tongue kiss.

Rodham drew back a couple inches. "I'm enjoying this while I can." He smiled, then went in for another deep kiss before they departed to their own apartments.

No one home. She laid her backpack on the table and strolled into the kitchen, pulling out a package of Bagel Bites. She spread them out and placed the cardboard tray in the microwave and took a couple steps to the fridge, snatching a water bottle. The door closed and she mindlessly stared at it while unscrewing the top of the water bottle, waiting for the microwave to beep. Her mother's schedule had today marked as off. *Where is she?*

The microwave beeped and she pulled the Bagel Bites out. Her mother always left her a note when she wasn't going to be home. She set her snack on the table and pulled her homework out of her backpack. Thoughts racing back to the night they slayed the Seekers. She'd been so preoccupied with supernatural awareness, battles, and new friends she hadn't thought much about her mother's recent absences from home.

Her mom pestered and urged her to get out of the house, explore, and make friends. She did, but was positive her mother wouldn't approve if she knew the danger they were in. Biting her upper lip, she shrugged. In Virginia, before her parents divorced, her mom had a girl's night out once a week. Maybe she'd found friends here. It wasn't wrong for her mother to have a social life, and since moving to St. Augustine all she'd done was work and come home.

Mindlessly, she worked through a series of trigonometry problems while eating Bagel Bites before her phone rang. Digging it from the backpack pocket, she noted the message light blink but ignored it to talk with her bestie in Virginia, Vicky. She missed her and was dying to talk with her.

"Hey Vic, switching over to camera, hold on." Alison touched the video icon and stood her phone up against her book.

Vicky's face lit up like a light bulb. "OMG, my parents are buying me a plane ticket to visit you for Thanksgiving!"

Alison's amber eyes enlarged into garnet spheres. "You serious?"

"Yeah! While I'm there we are checking out Flagler College!" Since Alison told her all about the weird Slayer stuff, Vicky was determined not to live vicariously through Alison but to join her and the terror in St. Augustine. A year ahead of Alison in school, she was a senior this year. "I get to see you and meet Rodham!" her voice bubbled on the other end.

The two girls squealed and exchanged ideas for plans during Vicky's visit. A couple hours later they hung up, the creepy feeling returned to Alison's guts and she felt as though she was being watched. She jumped out of her chair, nearly knocking it to the floor. It wobbled, then righted itself. She rushed into the kitchen and grabbed her mother's small hammer that she used for hanging pictures. It was small but, with a little force, could do some damage.

Hoisting it over her head, she crept into her mother's room, checking her closet and bathroom, then crept across the living room to her own bed and bath. Finding nothing, she drifted into the living room and yanked open the laundry room door and coat closet. Nothing. She closed them, letting her hammer hand go slack. Nobody was there.

She blew out a deep breath, bit her upper lip, and crunched her eyes. A note lay on the railing beside the front door. Alison scanned the room and glanced at the front door then the sliding glass door. Both were locked. The note hadn't been there when she got home, she'd have noticed it.

Cautiously she walked towards it. Laying the hammer beside it on the railing. A small red lady bug crawled towards the door. She scooped it up and opened the door, watching it spread its tiny wings and fly off. Closing the door, she picked up the note.

Her eyes widened. She'd checked the entire apartment and hadn't found anyone. *Was the note there when she entered the apartment?* If so, she hadn't seen it. Her blood rushed cold then a key jingled on the other side of the door and the knob turned. Her heart thumped against her chest until her mom walked through the doorway. The lights in the breezeway between the apartments were just coming to life.

Alison stuffed the note into her pocket. "Hi Mom," she said, relieved.

Her eyes shifted from Alison to the hammer. "Hi Al, why is my hammer laying on the railing?"

That's the first thing she said; not 'how was your day' or 'missed you' but why is my hammer not where it should be. Her mom was OCD about everything being in its place. Thinking quickly, she responded with a lame excuse but followed it with a slight guilt trip to dissolve the subject. "There was a nasty spider. I killed him and was just finishing cleaning his guts. Where were you?"

"Didn't you read my text?"

She remembered seeing the text alert but hadn't bothered to check it. "No… Vicky called and I got sidetracked with the nasty spider. She's coming for Thanksgiving!"

Her mom smiled and wrapped her arm around Alison's shoulder. "I know. I talked with her mom and we thought it would be a great idea."

"Really?"

She unwrapped her arm and strolled to the couch. "Don't act so surprised. Vicky is like a second daughter to me and I know how much you miss her."

Alison realized at that point that she'd been duped, not the other way around. Parents were tricky individuals.

"You want to watch a movie? Do like a girl's night?" suggested her mom, taking a seat on the couch and pulling off her shoes.

She plopped on the couch beside her. "Sure, sounds fun." They used to do movie nights a lot, but since moving and her mother working her crazy schedule at the hospital they didn't have much time together.

After a couple hours, night settled in and both grew tired. Alison didn't bother to attempt to pry information from her, choosing to simply enjoy the evening. In bed she checked her phone, her mother's message read *meeting a friend for an early dinner be home before dark.*

Her arm hairs prickled, then she reminded herself of her earlier mind conversation. She's allowed to have friends and be social. She slipped her pants off and, as they dropped to the floor, she spotted a corner of the mysterious note hanging out of her front pocket. Grabbing the end, she opened it.

I have information you're looking for. Meet me four p.m. tomorrow on the Fort lawn. I'll be wearing a Jaguar jersey and red ball cap.

Chapter 6

Mandy

Caly slowed her pace as they came to a large steel fence. Nothing but thick trees beyond it. "We're here. Climb off and follow me. Stay close," she ordered.

Mandy nodded as if Caly could see her as she climbed off her back. The violet haze in the atmosphere darkened. She felt bathed in its beauty and it excited everyelectron inside her. *Is this the light?* she questioned, but knew instinctively it was.

They walked along the fence for about a half mile before coming to a gate. Beyond the gate was a long road surrounded by dense woods and a path leading to a mansion. The violet light appeared to rise from behind the house.

It looked like something from an old horror movie. Tall columns supported an overhang to the double etched-glass front door and several levels jutted out with large balconies. The length of the house was the size of a mini mall and at the top was a rounded room with a large window. She imagined Rapunzel leaning her hair out the window for her to climb up then dismissed the silly thought.

When they got to the gate it slid open. Mandy followed Caly inside, her eyes gawking at the eerie place and mouth dropped open. The trail to the house was about another half mile. The porch was level with the ground. They walked onto it and the door opened for them.

A young woman stood on the other side. Her blonde hair falling over her chest in waves. She wore jeans and a plain red T-shirt. "Welcome to Wolf Manor, Mandy."

"How do you know my name...?" she asked, her voice drifting as she gaped at the shiny wood floors and antler chandelier, larger than her, hanging just above their heads. She wondered how many deer donated their lives for the tacky light fixture. The walls were built of rounded logs. The inside reminded her of a very detailed Lincoln Log home.

The young woman smiled. "You're famous around here so get used to it. We've been waiting sixteen years for your return."

Mandy had a ton of questions to ask and words dropped from her mouth like Niagra Falls.

Caly chuckled and the young blonde woman smiled then spoke. "Slow down. Carlito will answer everything. For now, let me show you to your room where you can freshen up and change clothes. I'll have our cook bring you in something to eat. I imagine you're famished."

Mandy's stomach roared at the mention of food and she followed the girl to a staircase and up the steps. Caly followed behind and turned to the left when they got to the second floor.

"What's your name?" Mandy asked.

The girl turned her head, pushing her hair over her shoulder so Mandy saw her full, flawless cheek.

"Oh my gosh. Well, that was rude of me. I'm Miranda."

They walked past several doors, all closed. Mandy wondered if anybody else lived here. A million rooms, but she'd seen no one except Caly and Miranda since they arrived.

They finally stopped in front of one of the many closed doors, Miranda opened it. "This is your suite. Umm..." she wrinkled her nose, "I handpicked all the clothes, so I hope they fit your taste. It was short notice, so let me know if you need anything else."

Mandy glimpsed the room. A huge bed, large enough to get lost in, was against the wall to her left. Across the expansive room was a wardrobe and tall dresser. In the middle was a pale blue suede love seat and matching chair. Between them stood a glass top table with a candle burning. It filled the room with a tropical scent.

Her eyes wide, she glanced toward Miranda. "All this is for me?"

Miranda nodded.

"But what if I'm not who you think I am?" she questioned, either out of attempting to maintain her sanity or simply denial.

"You are exactly who we think you are. You even look like her..." she said, then shut her mouth abruptly as if she'd said something she shouldn't.

"My birth mother?" asked Mandy.

Miranda pursed her lips and smiled.

Instead of hounding her, she changed the subject. "When will Joel be here?"

"Soon. By the time you shower and eat he should be arriving. Do you want me to send him up when he gets here?"

Send him up. Am I a prisoner? Mandy kept her thoughts to herself. "Yes please."

"Okee Doke." Miranda said and turned on her heels, exiting the room.

Mandy, alone with her thoughts, didn't want to think about all the weird crap and she didn't want to think about her mother. Visions of her lying on the floor in her own blood flashed across her mind repeatedly. She twisted at the many vibrant bands hanging against her wrist. She was curious to explore the house and find the place with the mysterious violet light, but first she wanted a shower. Residue from the cave creature still lingered around her neck.

After her shower, she dressed in fresh clothes. Stylish faded jeans that wrapped themselves around her legs and butt as if made for her and a simple cream blouse that hung longer in the back than the front. On the floor of the closet were a few pairs of cowboy boots. She'd never been a fan. Shrugging, she grabbed a cute pair with white fringe and slid them onto her socked feet. They were a perfect fit. She had to admit, Miranda had great taste in clothes.

On the glass table was a BLT and a glass of ice water. Her stomach grumbled and complained when she saw it. She was so hungry she could eat the whole thing in one bite.

She sat on the suede sofa and grabbed the sandwich, leaning and holding the plate over the floor. She didn't want to dirty the sofa, knowing it cost a bundle. Her mouth watered and all the flavors swirled in her mouth as she took a bite then another.

A knock on the door pulled her out of her food orgy.

"Man," said Joel's voice.

"Come in," she mumbled with a mouth full of food.

The door opened and the scent of body wash and aftershave hit her nose. She turned and watched him stroll towards her, freshly showered. His long damp hair hung against his cheeks with his single unruly curl jutting out.

He took a seat beside her. "This is where I grew up. Carlito is our Alpha. Once everyone is cleaned up we'll head downstairs."

"I was wondering if anyone actually lives in this huge house. It's like a ghost mansion."

He chuckled. "The guards in our pack live here, mostly single wolves with no family yet. They were on duty until we had you here safe. The guards are switching now. He'll keep a few more than usual on prowling the grounds but you'll meet most of them soon."

She stuffed the last bite of BLT into her mouth as he explained more about the werewolves.

Approximately an hour later, they headed down the stairs. She followed him through the area she'd entered and to a large room filled with wolves in human form. She glanced from one to the next. They parted and bowed their heads, making room for her and Joel to pass. When they reached the other end of the room they were greeted by a tall, well-built older man. His long black hair looked like silk as it fell to his shoulders, and his brown eyes were as dark as Joel's.

"Welcome Mandy," he said, in a deep voice. "I'm Carlito and this is the southeast wolf pack." He spread out his arms towards the many werewolves behind them, their heads still bowed.

"I know you have many questions and I have all the answers but they will have to wait. We have something more important to attend to first."

What could be more important? she thought. They carried her across the country to this mansion, told her she's something special and her parents are witches. They take her from her home, running from evil forces, fight them off in the woods and now it all has to wait. She bit her tongue and forced a smile. This man exuded confidence and leadership, she didn't want to offend him or bring shame to her deceased mother who'd taught her better than to disrespect elders.

Joel took her hand and squeezed it, then circled around her and guided her towards the doorway. He leaned in and whispered into her ear, "We have a funeral to attend."

Chapter 7

read gripped her guts. *Did one of them die trying to protect me?* Goosebumps raced up her arms, causing the hair to prickle. "Did... did one of them die because of me?"

He shifted his eyes towards her and a single tear escaped the corner of his right eye. "Selenia."

Her mouth formed an O. Their mother -- not that they were blood related, but his mother raised her as her own until yesterday. She didn't know until then she wasn't really her daughter, biologically anyway. In every other way she was. *Does that mean Joel is my brother?* The tear rolled down his cheek and landed on his shoulder.

No, they weren't siblings. Another wave of anger took siege of her. *How the heck did her body get here? Why didn't he tell me?* She swallowed hard to squash her thoughts and tightened her lips. They walked into the night air, the violet haze settled over them, lighting everything, and soothed her enough she asked in an even voice, "I don't get it, how did she get here?"

"The light witches transported her body as soon as we exited the house."

She thought back to the light ball that blew one of her attackers apart. *A light witch?* It made sense. Everything made sense, even though it shouldn't, and the damn violet light felt like home. There was far more going on and whatever the reason she was brought here the light was a big part of it. She felt it in every chemical bond within her body. "You knew this and didn't tell me?"

"No, I didn't. I didn't want to add to everything else you need to process."

Mandy calmed, soaking in the radiance as they walked through the woods. Its power enveloped her and she felt invincible in its glow. Small bugs with green lights glowed in the bushes and leaves adding to the surreal ambience of Wolf Manor. For what felt like a mile or so they continued deep into the woods until they reached a clearing surrounded by torches placed in a circular pattern. A few wolves stood inside the circle of torches.

Inside their circle lay a familiar body, her mother, and all the surreal moments from the past forty-eight hours froze. Reality seized her; never would her mother hold her again or give her advice. Mandy would never return to their house, they'd never again live their quiet life. This was her life now, surrounded by werewolves with nowhere to go and no one to go to, except Joel. Tears erupted from her eyes as she plodded closer to the middle of the circle.

She and Joel stopped, Selenia lying at their feet. The wolves around them each grabbed a torch and Carlito entered the circle with Joel and Mandy. He chanted in a language she didn't understand, his words chorused by the other wolves. A fog rose above her mother's body and took the shape of a wolf as it rose into the air.

Mandy choked back her sobs as she watched it drift high above the trees. Her mother's spirit was free. She didn't need to be a werewolf to understand what just happened. Her mother was free and it eased her soul. When she looked down to where her mother lay it was empty except for a pile of dirt.

Carlito cleared his throat and shifted his eyes to Mandy and Joel. "Pick up a handful of dirt and blow it in the direction of the wind so her remains will cover the land."

They did as he asked then everyone placed their torches back on pedestals and solemnly retreated towards the house. Mandy took one last glance at the spot her mother's body had lain. From the corner of her eye she saw a violet shadow move through the tree line. Joel squeezed her hand, urging her onward. She squeezed back and walked in step with him behind all the wolves, their heads bowed in silence. The ceremony, although strange, was beautiful in its simplicity.

Mandy wanted to chase the mysterious violet shadow but didn't want to disrespect her mother. Inside, she knew she'd made the right choice and peace rested on her soul. When they entered the mansion, the entire group moved into a large room with a feast of food. Every type of meat -- rare, extremely rare -- and rolls, potatoes, biscuits, gravies.

Beer flowed freely, country rock played loud, and she hunted for fruit, since she disliked near-raw meat, but it was futile so she settled on eating a couple rolls. The wolves mingled. She stuck to Joel's side until Miranda and another female wolf every bit as perfect and gorgeous found her. They looked like sisters. Blonde hair fell across their backs and shoulders in waves and both had bright blue round eyes surrounded by oval faces.

"The clothes OK?" asked Miranda, a smile across her face.

Mandy chuckled. "They're perfect," she responded, enjoying how they fit her like a glove.

"They look good and the way Joel looks at you, he noticed it too," said the other wolf. Mandy recognized her voice as Caly. She was just as gorgeous in human form as wolf form.

Wrinkling her nose and lifting a brow she asked, "Really?" Now the cat was out of the bag. She should have left it alone. Her entire opinion of Joel was changing and the idea of him noticing her too was overwhelming.

Caly and Miranda nodded in unison. "He's a total hottie!" said Miranda.

Caly smiled as she elbowed Miranda.

She knew it would sound stupid, or she thought it would, but had to ask anyways, "Are you sisters?"

They smiled. "A year apart."

They talked for a bit and she thought to ask them about the light but chose against it. Tonight belonged to her mother.

"You want to go riding tomorrow?" asked Caly. "The grounds are beautiful and there's so much to show you."

Miranda and Caly smiled at her with a pleased look in their eyes, she couldn't refuse and was dying to explore. Maybe she could even trust these girls. She wanted to.

Speaking of Joel, she looked around and didn't see him anywhere. She didn't see Carlito either.

"Our largest celebrations are funerals. We believe in celebrating life and we're standing here like wall flowers. Let's dance," said Caly, taking her hand. Miranda took the other.

She decided to forget about Joel and weird mystery stuff. They were right; it was a time to celebrate her mother's life.

Hours later, Joel joined her. She didn't bother to ask where he'd been. Caly and Miranda were a ton of fun and she was tired and ready to drop onto her bed. He walked her to her room and they said goodnight.

After tossing and turning, her molecules too stirred for a good night's sleep, she scooted out of bed, opened her door and peered into the hallway. The coast clear, she tiptoed up the stairs. It was more an instinct that drove her up them with only moonlight to guide her way. She gripped the railing as she took one step at a time. The house was eerily quiet for having so many wolves living inside it.

Two flights later, she made it to the top. To her right was empty space with large windows on either side, moonlight bathing the area. She tried to remember how many floors she'd counted when she first saw the place, but couldn't remember, or maybe she hadn't counted at all.

Regardless, she explored the open area. The vaulted ceiling gave the space a larger appearance

than it actually was, although it was still sizable --
about the size of the entire house she grew up in. It
lacked furniture and décor. Soon, satisfied nothing
was there, she strolled to one of the windows that
covered half the wall space.

Miles of trees spread out before her, and
between them were empty patches. The mixture of
moonlight and violet haze made it easy for her to
see. They weren't empty patches but groupings of
houses like little villages. She remembered Joel said
only the single guards lived in the mansion. The
whole community continued to amaze her. *So who
lived outside the house? The ones with families*, she
answered her own question and decided she really
needed to learn more about werewolf hierarchy and
traditions.

The haze, more of a glow at that altitude, called
to her. She had to find where it was coming from.
She pressed her face against the window and shifted
her eyes upwards and around. To her right was the
circular Rapunzel tower. The violet glow swirled
around it as if coming from something inside, but
there were no more stairs. For the life of her she
hadn't a clue how to get to it. Defeated, she
shrugged and let out a large breath of air, then
headed towards the stairs. Scanning the room one
last time, she noted a light purple haze. She lifted an
eyebrow and strode towards it.

She hadn't noticed it before, probably because
she wasn't looking. The muted light eddied into the
center of the room and mixed with the moon's
beams. She stood dead center inside the focal point

of all the rays. Lifting her arms she twirled in it, soaking it up like a human sponge. A burst of energy surged through her core upwards and a warm electricity buzzed inside her. Identical to the strange rush she felt when she instinctively placed her hands upon her mother causing her to shoot upwards with a second wind. .

Is this my power? I soak up radiation and light? It made a bizarre kind of unexplainable sense, but what on Earth did she do with it? The energy was trapped inside her, vibrating like a million bouncy rubber balls.

A long sliver of violet caught the corner of her eye while she pondered the power growing inside her. She halted her spin and followed the light with her eyes, then paused when she caught sight of her arm. The violet light glowed from inside her. Her whole body shone like a Christmas bulb. She shifted from side to side and watched it move with her in psychedelic swirls.

A thump sounded above, grabbing her attention, and she refocused on the light. It radiated from the wall furthest from her. Curious, she followed it and ran her finger along the wall. It was the tiniest crack, barely perceptible even to her touch, that ran from the floor to the ceiling, straight, like a hidden door.

She pushed against it with her palms and felt for a knob or latch. She wasn't getting this close and giving up. Resting herself against the wall, she let out a deep breath. Tiny vibrations bounced against the wall. She pushed her ear against it and heard muffled voices and footsteps moving in her direction but she couldn't tear herself away. Whatever was in there, she desired it. *Follow the light* chorused inside her from every tiny, bouncing, rubber ball.

The light is mine! What are they hiding? She remembered Joel telling her about her birth and how important she was for humanity and the violet shadow moving through the woods after her mother's funeral. *Is it something mystical they keep trapped in the tower? Or someone?*

A sudden bolt of pain blasted through her head. She gripped her face and crumpled to the floor in a lump. Clutching her middle, the pain subsided as the light inside her exited through her fingertips and vanished.

With no time to bolt downstairs and nowhere to hide she stayed crumpled on the floor a few feet away along the wall in the shadows. The wall-door opened without a sound and the brilliant light bathed the room. With every ounce of her being she fought the urge to run through the opening and capture it. She clenched her jaws and eyes to control her urges. A light-hearted whistling and gentle footsteps padded across the room.

She unclenched her eyes and watched Carlito exit. Not once did he look her direction. The door closed. She'd given up her chance, but knew she didn't have the strength to take down an alpha wolf.

Chapter .8

Alison and the Slayers

Alison stood on the fort's – Castillo de San Marcos National Monument large expanse of lawn, a breeze from the bay blowing her pony tail over her eyes. She wrapped it up and forced the ends through her scrunchie. Her eyes scanning for a Jaguar Jersey and red cap.

Rodham stood near the fort, Lacey near S. Castillo Dr., and Adrian near Matanzas Bay. They decided as a group it was best for Alison to meet with the mystery person alone so it wouldn't spook him/her, yet they felt they needed to be close in case he/she wasn't to be trusted. Lacey still had her amulet and was getting far better at using its power. One telekinetic swipe and she could fling the mystery person into the bay.

Finally, she spotted the red ball cap approaching from Adrian's direction. She moved towards the mystery person as she crossed the large expanse of lawn. She recognized him as the older man who'd answered the door at Veronica's house, chin fat flapping as he walked. *So he does know something?* Since killing Bloodseekers she'd become far more confident and brave, although butterflies still flittered in her belly. She fought the urge to glance toward Rodham, not wanting to alert the old man.

He tipped his hat as he approached. "I first need to apologize. When you came to my door I didn't know who you were. My name is Tim."

"Alison," she said, shielding her eyes from the sun.

"Your friends might as well join us. What I have to say they also need to hear." He smiled as he waved towards Lacey.

Alison smiled. She didn't think they stuck out. *How does he know?* Other things were more important. "How did you get into my apartment?"

He nodded, his face changing before her. His skin tightening, the bags in his neck smoothed tight and the wrinkles disappeared. Before her stood a man who looked to be in his early twenties.

"What the—" she said, jumping back.

He smiled. "You might as well know there's more out there than Bloodseekers and Slayers. I'm a Shiftling. I have the ability to change into almost any form, so long as it's that of a living thing."

Alison blew out a large breath followed by a sigh. "Shiftling. Well if witches and Bloodseekers exist, why not? Do you have any werewolf friends? Maybe elf neighbors?" the sarcastic edge in her tone surprised even her.

He stared at her unfazed. "Elves -- not to my knowledge. Werewolves -- yes, but not here. They don't interact with the outside world much."

Then the Shiftling idea smacked her brain so hard the words flew out her mouth, "You shifted into a lady bug to get into my apartment!" She'd read all about shifters, werewolves, and held the hope that they didn't really exist as vampires and witches do, but she was dead wrong.

"A harmless lady bug and I came in on your backpack."

Adrian approached first, followed by Rodham, with Lacey on his heels.

"Let's walk," he suggested. The four of them listened to his wild story about very important twins being born on werewolf grounds. The first one born, Veronica, was sent to live with him and his mate. The second one born was sent to live with a werewolf in an undisclosed location. The wolves and shifters are distant cousins, both having genetic anomalies that make it possible for their bodies to change form.

The twins' father was a night witch and their mother a light witch. That made sense to her, since Veronica was able to cloak her mind, yet used light witch powers to slay Seekers. The twins were taken from their parents and separated for their own protection. The belief is if these sisters find each other and combine their powers with the Slayers, they could cure the world. Alison didn't know about that, but she did remember how Veronica's power accentuated theirs, so the possibility was real.

It was the last couple years that Veronica learned she had powers. The local Shiftlings kept close eyes on her but didn't interfere, as her nature was to kill Slayers not defend them. "We began to wonder if she was the light sister and not the dark as predicted," he said. They let her powers develop on their own and were awed by her abilities.

When he finally cut to the chase, Tim told them he believes she was taken by a night witch, Arama, and hidden beneath the city in a series of tunnels used in the past that travel from Jacksonville to St. Augustine to be brainwashed or used as bait to lure her sister to the sorceress herself; the mother of all Bloodseekers.

When he finished talking Rodham asked, "Where is the other sister?"

Tim rubbed his chin. "She's coming."

Lacey lifted an eyebrow. "Why are they so special, and what exactly does this have to do with us?"

"You are. I mean, from what I know if you're in a light witch bloodline you either are a witch or a Slayer," he said with irritation in his voice.

"Hold on one minute," Alison nearly shouted, "not everyone in our bloodlines is a witch or a Slayer and how do you know all this stuff?"

He voice changed from irritated to amused. "We supernaturals have to support one another. If the general population knew we existed there'd be chaos."

They all nodded in agreement.

"The same witch who kidnapped Veronica stole your amulets. If you help us, we'll help you. We can go anywhere without being noticed," his voice irritated and abrupt. "Having a group of teens assisting us isn't what I do for fun, but Veronica is important to me. We've raised her, and I want no harm to come her way. You'll have your amulets back to destroy nasty Bloodseekers and we'll have our girl."

"Give us a second," said Adrian, walking a few feet away from Tim and gathering the Slayers into a huddle. "I don't trust him, but we need our amulets and I hate to think Veronica is trapped somewhere being tortured. She may be a witch in every form of the word but she's our frenemy and helped us."

They agreed.

"You have a deal," Adrian said, the others nodding their heads in accordance.

Tim told them where to find the tunnels and that he'd be in contact with them soon. As they departed, Alison broke from the group and caught up to Tim. During their battle with the Bloodseekers, a group of dogs chasing a cat did an extreme amount of damage and saved their hides. After what Tim said she didn't think it was a coincidence anymore.

She had a suspicion that the Shiftlings had already helped them. "Err... you said you can shift into anything living. In the middle of our battle a group of dogs came out of nowhere chasing a cat. Was that Shiftlings?"

He chuckled. "You catch on quick. I'm being facetious. That was a group of Shiftlings. Like I said, we keep our eyes on her."

She understood where Veronica developed her charming personality from. This guy was as charming as a stump of wood. "Thanks." She ran back to the others who'd stopped and waited for her.

They needed a plan. She wasn't relying on him, or any Shiftling, to decide the fate of the Slayers.

Chapter 9

Mandy

Mandy awoke as the bright sunlight streamed across the room, causing a haze to blanket it in white. Joel's arm was draped over her chest. Instead of going back to her room where she'd be alone she heeded her mother's warning in the note and snuck into Joel's bed. She knew she could trust him and her gut said she could trust Caly and Miranda too, but she didn't know about Carlito, especially after what she saw last night. Something was up there, something that was hers and she was going to find out what or who.

She enjoyed the moment and his warm body next to hers. All the years she'd known him she'd loved him, but that love was changing into something else. An attraction that she wasn't sure what to do with. He was her upstairs neighbor and close family friend. Joel was also an attractive man. *Did I selectively ignore my attraction to him?*

He never ages, so how old is he? Will I age slowly too? If he has children with a non-werewolf will the offspring carry the gene? She couldn't believe the thoughts in her own mind. *Children?* She was several years from even considering it. The thought of them was absurd. He wasn't even attracted to her. She was his kid sister.

Or was he? Miranda and Caly seemed to think so. She shook the thought from her head.

He groaned and lifted his arm off her chest. "I'm sorry," he said in a hushed voice.

She turned to face him. "Don't be. I kinda liked it there." Her cheeks flushed -- that was too forward.

His cheeks turned three shades of pink. "Good morning. I didn't know you were here," he said, rising from the bed. His sweats hanging low around his waist.

"I couldn't sleep so I snuck in. I hope you don't mind," she said, rolling on her side to face him and tucking her hands beneath her head.

He stretched his arms over his head, ignoring her flirtatiousness. "Did you sleep?"

"Yeah."

"Then I don't mind," he responded, giving her a smile. His brown tufts stuck out in too many angles to count.

Joel headed towards his bathroom and Mandy hurried to her own room. She needed a shower and then breakfast. If she was exploring with the girls she needed energy.

She followed her nose to the kitchen. The mansion was designed with one staircase that went straight up. On the first floor was Carlito's office, the kitchen, living room, and the huge room they'd partied in after her mom's funeral. There was a set of doors that led to the outside, but she hadn't explored them; she was too busy dancing with Caly and Miranda. On every other floor were suites like hers, or so she thought.

In the kitchen was a long table with possibly a hundred chairs. It was filled with a spread of high starch and protein foods. She grabbed a couple slices of bacon, a biscuit, and piled gravy on top. She really wanted fresh fruit but none was available so she grabbed a glass of orange juice.

Maybe twenty wolves sat at the kitchen table, raw meat and loads of carbs heaped on their plates. Mandy took a seat by herself. She didn't know any of them and didn't know where to find Caly. Lucky for her she didn't have to.

"Good morning," said Caly as she sat down beside her. A rare steak and a gob of white stuff on her plate.

Mandy tilted her head, studying the creamy white gob. "Good morning."

"Sorry. We eat our meat extremely rare," she said with a toothy smile.

"It's not the meat. I'm used to that, so did my mom. What is the other stuff?"

"Grits," Caly answered as if Mandy should know what grits were.

She wrinkled her nose. "Grits. That doesn't sound appetizing."

Caly smiled and giggled. "They're amazing and a great source of carbs. We eat a high protein/carb diet for strength and energy."

Mandy nodded and picked at her breakfast.

"Try a bite," offered Caly.

She thought about it. What did she have to lose? She reached her fork over and dabbed at the grits then brought them to her mouth. "Not bad."

Caly lifted her brows. "Miranda will be down in a minute, are you ready to explore?"

Mandy's eyes shot up. "Heck yeah!" She wanted to ask her about the hidden room but couldn't find the words and thought it better to wait until they were out of Carlito's possible earshot. She didn't know how sensitive their hearing was, but figured it was that of actual wolves, at least in wolf form.

"Great! There's something I want to show you," replied Caly with wide eyes.

She trusted Caly after riding with her and she liked her personality and loved Miranda's taste in clothes. Caly and Miranda were two of the most beautiful women she'd ever seen. Despite their high carb/protein diet they had thin, muscular frames with medium curves in the right places. Their long blonde hair was thick, full, and shone like silk. Today, Caly wore hers pulled back in a long plait that trailed down her back, but yesterday it flowed freely. Her eyes as blue as Crater Lake in Oregon. They'd vacationed there once when she was five and her mother disappeared at night, leaving her in Joel's care. She understood now that she was letting her wolf out to run and hunt.

Miranda joined them and the three girls left. The sun was bright and the air chilly. Trees surrounded the grounds and a few distinct trails veered off in various directions through the woods. They stayed on the sidewalk that wrapped around the house. Mandy hadn't noticed it yesterday. The sidewalk curved around the house and Caly stopped. A series of garage doors spanned the entire side of the house.

Caly punched in a code on a pad and one of the doors opened. Inside was a series of dirt bikes and three wheelers.

"We don't always run," Caly said with a smirk. "You know how to drive one of these?"

Mandy shook her head. This place was full of surprises.

"No problem, you can ride with me." She started the engine of one of the three wheelers. "This one's mine, hop on."

Miranda boarded another three wheeler and pulled beside Caly.

Mandy approached from the rear and noted the small license plate *Calypso* in curvy letters. She chuckled inside. The werewolves were curious creatures. She tried to imagine her mom living here. Besides rare meat, she'd never seen an adventurous spirit inside her mother. She was always calm, rational, and predictable.

She scooted onto the seat and wrapped her arms around Caly's middle, remembering how firm it was, like Joel's. *Do these people have no fat on their bodies?* Her mom was always firm too. Was it their diet or the amount of exercise they received on a regular basis? Maybe it was the gene or set of genes.

They roared out of the garage and along one of the well-worn trails. Now she knew how the trails got there. To her surprise, the area was hilly. She hadn't even asked where she was. Through the chill she felt a moistness in the air that she'd never felt in Arizona. There were plenty of trees, no shortage of oxygen, and hilly areas that made Mandy's stomach flop as the three wheeler rushed over them.

The wind blowing through her hair and whipping her cheeks, being with this beautiful, vibrant woman, opened her to the sense of adventure and, coupled with the violet glow, she felt unstoppable and powerful. Tilting her head back, she allowed the wind to rush over her neck. The vehicle flew out of the woods to a clearing surrounded by houses. One of the small communities she'd seen from the window. Young children played outside and adults busied themselves with chores. Caly finally slowed and stopped the vehicle by a stream.

"This stream runs through the middle of our land," Caly said, pride in her voice.

"Wolf Manor is protected, others can't see it," announced Miranda with satisfaction, folding her arms over her chest.

Caly shot her a death glance. Mandy ignored the comment for the moment, "Where is Wolf Manor?"

"Tennessee, honey. The other side of the stream heads into Kentucky. You've only seen a small portion of our land. I love it out here," she said. "Let's take a walk, we have something to show you."

The threesome strolled along the water's edge. Beneath the stream's surface, aquatic life flourished.

Caly reached her hand upward towards a tree branch above her head and pulled a juicy red apple off it. "Here."

Mandy's eyes widened as she thankfully grabbed the apple from her and bit in. It was juicy and sweet. "How did you know?" she asked between bites.

"You didn't look thrilled with our spread of meat and bread," Miranda giggled. "We don't usually eat fresh fruit but use it for canning, fresh juice, that kind of thing." She pulled down a few more apples and placed them in a pile. "We'll take these back with us."

Mandy ate another as they chatted. The wolves in the villages had families and other jobs around Wolf Manor; hunting, maintaining the grounds, cleaning and cooking inside the large house, gardening and a variety of all the other things that kept Wolf Manor running smoothly. Family wolves were encouraged to stay out of the guard and tend their families. At thirteen, a Wolf shifted for the first time during the first full moon after their birthday. At that point they joined the guard and their aging process went from normal human years to very slow.

Mandy bit her lip as she listened and they cozied to her. Now was possibly the only time she'd have them to herself and curiosity was killing her. No Carlito, nothing but fresh air, she popped the question resting on her brain, "You said the land is protected?"

Caly narrowed her eyes as Miranda spoke, "I shouldn't have said it. The light witches placed wards and spells around the outside of the grounds. Regular humans can't find it."

"What about non-regular humans?" she asked with a dash of trepidation in her voice.

"Most of them can't see it either," she said as she twirled a small tree branch between her fingers.

Mandy had stumbled on something she shouldn't have and the tension between them sat in the air like a big white elephant. To lighten the mood she giggled, "It's really pretty. I can see why." She knew it wasn't the beauty or the ambience. It had something to do with the darn violet light hanging over the land.

She'd plucked their brains enough and didn't want to lose friends before she made them.

After spending the morning in the woods, they returned. Mandy ran upstairs to her room and showered. She then plodded downstairs for another high carb/high protein meal but, to her surprise, a fruit salad awaited her. She gazed at Caly who gave her a wink from across the room.

Joel joined her. After eating a raw slab of meat, he turned towards Mandy. "Carlito is ready to see us."

Chapter 10

A week later
Alison and the Slayers

Alison did her research and found no underground tunnels in St. Augustine. She scratched her head in confusion. The Bloodseekers lived underground and sometimes above ground but had for many years survived beneath the surface of St. Augustine. If they lived underground there had to be passages and tunnels they used to travel and Tim told them the tunnels connected St. Augustine and Jacksonville. He even told them how to get there.

Plugging in tunnels beneath North Florida a ton of websites came up. One by one she searched through them. Each indicated there was a series of tunnels beneath Jacksonville -- St. Augustine's neighbor city to the north.

According to the articles, they were used to transport passengers, others were used by banks to store money. There were even old vaults. Her mind pieced together, *if these passenger tunnels exist they had to transport people somewhere so do they reach to St. Augustine?* She continued reading the article and learned they were filled with four feet of water.

Swishing her lips back and forth, then biting her top lip, she blew up her cheeks and let out a large breath of air and switched gears. She remembered what the sarcastic Shiftling Tim said 'from what I know if you're in a light witch bloodline you either are a witch or a Slayer.' But that wasn't true -- her mom wasn't a witch, none of the Slayers' parents were witches but they do all have magic in their blood line. The amulets were spelled and that gave them their abilities. So did their abilities only come from the amulets or did they have magic that made the amulets work? Not just anyone could be a Slayer, only specific individuals, and they skipped generations.

Is it a specific gene passed down that carried the magic -- a group of genes, or did everyone in the bloodline have the ability of magic in some way but it lay dormant until triggered? It was worth a try. She knew she could develop her skill but to what level could she hide herself? *Can I cloak myself from humans and witches?* Her brain hurt, she needed to bounce her ideas off someone. She first thought to call Gran, but decided against it. Gran was aging rapidly and she needed to learn to tackle these problems with the other Slayers, so she called Lacey.

Once Lacey answered, she put her on video cam and explained her thinking.

Lacey beamed. "Hold up. Are you thinking of exploring the tunnels?"

"Yup," Alison replied, then bit her lip. She'd had better ideas, but at the moment this seemed like the only option.

"Hmm... I can push the water back, but I don't know how long I can hold it."

"But if we have other magic beyond what the amulets give us... maybe Adrian and Rodham can help hold the water," Alison stated. She lifted herself up on one elbow and propped the phone against a pillow on her bed.

"Even if that's possible, what about you? You're not invisible to witches and if the night witch is down there with Veronica you won't be protected." Lacey's eyes expanded and streaks of yellow flashed across the blue of her irises

"I'm thinking the magic will allow me to cloak myself from her."

Lacey raised an eyebrow. "You think it will?"

"I don't know, but it's worth a try." Truly, she wanted to snuggle in bed with a good book and let someone else save the world, but it was laid on her shoulders and those of the other Slayers. It was time she stopped being a chicken.

They both sat quiet for several seconds, then Lacey had a sudden brainstorm. "Are you picking me up for the game tonight? You can practice there."

Alison rolled the idea around in her head. "That's a brilliant idea!"

Lacey's lips curled in a smile. "Get off the phone. You need to get dressed. Those ratty sweats won't do."

Alison clicked off the phone. Lacey was a fashion freak and Alison couldn't care. Clothes were clothes. The whole idea of friends -- plural -- was new to her. She dug through her closet until she found a decent pair of shorts and a blouse that Lacey wouldn't cringe over. Rodham, on the other hand, didn't care. They'd had enough mind conversations that she knew.

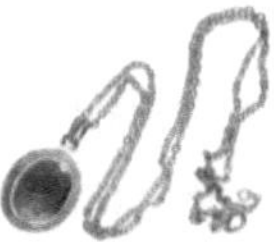

Alison concentrated hard, focusing all the amulet's energy into her until she felt a rush of electricity buzz through her veins. She walked up behind another student and bumped into them. The girl turned around and scowled. "Watch where you're going." She looked her square in the eye.

Alison apologized and went back to Lacey. "It's not working." She dropped to the bleacher.

"That's only the third person. You can't give up yet. Let's brainstorm. What are you doing internally?"

Lacey the optimist. Alison sighed and responded, "I'm working my energy into a frenzy so it buzzes through my entire body."

"Maybe you should do the opposite. Let your body relax. Stop the energy from moving."

Alison let her body go and tried to stop the movement, including all thoughts in her mind.

"Are you relaxed?" Lacey said in an excited voice, making Alison jump and forcing her out of deep relaxation.

"I was..."

"Oops, sorry," Lacey responded, wrinkling her nose. "I'm thirsty, gonna grab a sweet tea. Do you want anything?"

"No thanks."

Alison watched Lacey stroll toward the concession stand. She had a natural finesse and bubbliness about her that Alison admired. When she walked in a room, people noticed. She effervesced in a way Alison knew she never would. She was like a blast of sunshine, literally! Lacey and her BF, Vicki in Virginia, had a lot in common. She wondered how they'd get along when Vicki visited for Thanksgiving. Would they get along so well they forgot about her? She kicked herself mentally for thinking that.

A shock of electricity shot through her body as someone sat on the bench beside her, brushing her hand.

Immediately she turned. A good-looking guy, in a surfer kind of way, was sitting next to her. His straight long blond hair hung shoulder length. He had a cute dimple on the right side of his mouth and brown eyes that twinkled unnaturally.

"I overheard your conversation. I wasn't eavesdropping. I was sitting a row back and have sensitive hearing. I can help you."

Alison blinked, unsure what to say. The electricity that buzzed through her body from his touch put him in one category -- a supe. But was he another Slayer? If so, he didn't glow. Maybe a witch or something else. Until the other day she didn't know anything else existed, but now she knew about Shiftlings and werewolves.

His smile didn't waver as he brought his hand between them and light sparked from his fingertips.

"You're a light witch," she whispered in awe.

He nodded. "It sounds like you and your friend need one."

How much did he hear? Before she finished her thought he grabbed her hands. Energy excited her molecules and zipped through her body. She recognized the feeling and wasn't shocked when he let go of her hands and they were behind the stadium in the field where she first learned Veronica was a witch.

"It's more private here. We don't need people listening to us. And your friend is on her way," he said with a grin.

"What?" she said before she remembered witches were telepathic. "Never mind," she followed up with.

"I'm Cody."

"Alison."

Within a few minutes Lacey joined them, jumping right into it and getting to the point. "I'm so happy you found us. We could use you on our side."

He smiled. "My parents are powerful witches. As their offspring, I have a collection of all their powers; telekinesis, telepathy, lighting balls and bolts, teleportation, and pretty much anything. Anyone in a witch bloodline has magic, but it has to be practiced."

Lacey stomped her foot and folded her arms over her chest. "You've known about us. You see our glow, so why didn't you come to us sooner?"

He chuckled. "I'm a witch. I know this is new to you, but we don't get involved unless you need us. We created Slayers. One person, every other generation in a witch of the light bloodline, that the spelled amulets call to and who can use the magic inside the amulet."

Alison rolled the idea around in her head. That wasn't news, but she grasped again at the light witch bloodline thing. A thought clung to her brain and manifested. They didn't derive all their power from the amulets. They each had magic inside them that accentuated the magic in the amulet.

Lacey twisted her face. "You can help us?

"I can help you draw on your own magic that makes the magic in the amulets stronger. Don't get me wrong, you won't be able to share each other's magic unless you are connected by touch but you can strengthen the spelled magic in the amulets and do most anything with it," he paused.

"I don't know if you've felt it, but there's disturbance in our energy field. Something big is happening, coming our way. We need to be prepared and ready and you need to tap into powers that other Slayers naturally tap into overtime. You don't have that time," he said, his face and voice grave.

Chapter 11

Mandy

Carlito was mysteriously called away to take care of some type of werewolf stuff, so Mandy never had the chance to hear what was so important or give him a piece of her mind. A week at Wolf Manor and her irritation was seething, begging to be released.

Joel was awesome as always, and most nights she snuck into his bed. It was the only way she could find the peace to rest. The molecules in her body stayed excited all day and all night, and feeling his heartbeat and slowed breathing soothed her enough to sleep.

She blamed it on the blasted violet light that begged and called to her. Each night she prowled the house, searching for another way into the tower room from where the light emanated. Pictures of werewolves hung along the walls and sconces with half-melted candles, and every night the eerie quiet gave her the creeps. The house was like something from a horror movie, something she'd expect to house supernatural creatures. But there appeared to be only one way into the Rapunzel tower. The secret door.

After exploring, she crawled into Joel's bed and snuggled against him until she fell asleep. After a week, he expected her to sneak into his room.

Mandy plopped onto her sofa. She felt like a prisoner and couldn't leave the grounds. The only saving grace was Joel and becoming close to Miranda and Caly. She was a prisoner of what she thought of as "The Compound". *You're special. We need to protect you,* her mind mocked as she clutched her fists so tight her fingernails drew blood from her palms. She didn't call it that in front of any wolves so as not to disrespect them, yet each day her respect and feeling of being a prisoner grew. If she didn't do something soon she'd rage on all of them.

Not giving the drops of blood dripping from her hand any mind, she lifted the orange juice to her lips and took a large swallow. It was sweet as it drained down her throat. She set the glass on the table. She needed a plan. Strolling to the window, the sun set; reds and oranges mingled with the perpetual violet. She turned and closed the curtains, realizing for the first time how heavy they were as her fingers lingered on the edge.

She turned it over and studied the fabric on the side facing out. Twisting it between her fingers, she felt a layer between the fabrics of the curtain. They blocked out the purple light, most of it, from the inside of the house. It was muted most in her suite. She'd known that, but even with the light blocked it was inside her -- not only her head, but in every atom of her being.

Mandy cut along the seam with scissors from the bathroom, separating the fabric from the flexible, strong layer. It was lead; like the tech laid over her when she broke her arm as a child. *Is it meant to keep me from the light? Do they think they've successfully blocked me from it?* She sneered at the thought.

The light was for her. Every day its message to her became louder and more urgent. It needed her to find it. Someone was in trouble, a half to her whole, the bearer of the phantom pains like the one that sucked the light and power out of her and her finding that light was the key to their salvation. Why or how she didn't know, only that she needed to capture it before she left The Compound. Tonight.

A knock on her door startled her from her thoughts.

"It's Joel. Can I come in?"

"Yeah," she answered in a weak, defeated voice.

He sat down next to her. "You've been hiding in here all day. Is everything alright?"

She hadn't yet told him how she felt and considered if she should. The concern in his brown eyes was unmistakable, but did she trust him? He'd been her neighbor all her life but she was rethinking everything she knew. *Can I still trust him?* He'd brought her there and both he and his mother had hidden their werewolf nature. She recited the words in her mother's note mentally. She had to trust Joel, yet cringed. She was somehow important, but not enough for Carlito to explain before leaving indefinitely. She decided if she didn't say something soon she'd explode from the darn violet light filling her up inside. "I'm... uh... going stir crazy."

He leaned back against the sofa and rested his arm on the back of it and against her neck. "Me too. I've been gone so long that I miss the outside world. It's not safe to leave, but why don't we explore Wolf Manor together?"

She turned her head and took in his profile. His strong jaw line and five o'clock shadow drove her crazy! She desired nothing more than to feel his lips pressed against hers. "That sounds fun. Maybe it'll get me out of my funk."

He stood abruptly, causing her to bounce, and grabbed her hands, catching her as the bounce lifted her into the air. She didn't think she'd ever get used to his werewolf speed. All the years she'd known him and his mother, her adopted mother, they lived by human standards. It blew her mind they'd done it for her. It was a sacrifice she was only beginning to understand. They defied their nature and she imagined he must feel relieved to not have to be something he wasn't any longer.

They walked into the woods. He dropped his clothes and shifted into his wolf form. She grabbed his pile of clothes and jumped on his back. Here he was free. Could she ask him to leave this? Did she want to leave him? The only reason she hadn't attempted to scale the fence was the wolves who not only prowled inside the grounds but outside. She wasn't faster than them and they'd soon catch her and bring her back. She also needed the annoying light. Well, that's what she told herself. Her dark tresses of hair caught in the wind as she rode him. She knew Joel was the real reason.

She could bust the secret door and grab the darn light, but could she leave him?

He stopped in front of one of the cabins and she climbed off his back. His body shifted and, within seconds, a naked Joel stood before her. She blushed as she tried not to stare at his perfect abs and other parts.

"Not used to it yet?" he asked with a smile of confidence.

She wrinkled her nose and elbowed his firm chest playfully.

He walked toward the cabin and opened the door. "This is the cabin we lived in. It's vacant now."

She followed him inside. It was cozy and rustic. The walls and vaulted ceiling -- stained wood. Two wooden-framed chairs and a matching sofa sat in front of a fireplace. To their left were two doors and to the right another door and a kitchen area surrounded by a bar with three barstools.

She imagined Joel as a young boy growing up in this simple, warm, inviting cabin and she wondered what happened to his father. She'd never asked him and didn't get the chance to ask her mother. When she asked about her father, she said he passed away. *Was she referring to her real father or Joel's father?* It was all getting so confusing. "Can I ask you a personal question?"

Joel dressed in his clothes then rested a few logs in the fireplace. "Shoot."

"What about your father?"

He released his squat and rested his butt against the floor on a furry rug. "My father was a leader among the wolves and highly respected," he took in a deep breath. "I'm far older than I look -- we all are. It was over a century ago when his life was taken. I was very young and don't remember him well. My mother always told me I reminded her of him."

"Selenia." She cleared her throat and pulled a pillow off the sofa, grasping it against her chest for warmth against the rigid chill in the cabin as she sat next to him on the floor.

He nodded. "As I mentioned, the wolves don't like to get involved with business not their own or part of the outside world, but sometimes it's unavoidable."

A shiver ran up her spine as she listened.

"A group of wolves, my father included, were investigating strange activities to the southeast that caught their attention and disrupted their peace on this land. Unknowing, they were caught in a supernatural battle between a group of teens known as Slayers and Bloodseekers. The wolves were ambushed by the Bloodseekers. One of the Slayers, the healer, found them but not in enough time to save them all. Carlito's life was saved, but when she got to my father it was too late." His eyes stared at the floor as he smoothed the fur rug beneath him.

She shivered again, an eerie feeling crept into her gut. At first she thought it was down to his haunting story but it was something more. Something about the house brought flashes of memory and a settling urge to tear the cabin apart. There was something in it she needed, something Selenia hid for her. "I'm sorry." She paused then asked, "Did I ever live here?"

He nodded. "Only for a few days. Why?"

"I feel like I've been here and… Never mind." She closed her mouth and stared at the logs in the fireplace.

The air filled with silence as he lit the few pieces of wood. "You seem unsettled inside the house. I thought we could spend the night here. We can even move in if you'd like."

Stay for the night? Move in? Is he talking about permanently? She was attracted to him. More than that, she desired him in a way that even she didn't understand. But live here with him, stay on these lands? She couldn't. She had to get the light and leave. Confusion muddled her brain.

As he rested against the chair, she leaned her back against his firm chest. He lifted her hair and the frosty air nipped at her neck until he laid it down, running his fingers over it. The sensation of his touch on her head sent signals of desire rushing through her.

She wanted to stay there as he caressed her and forget everything, but she couldn't. Lifting her chest suddenly, she scooted around and looked him in the eye. An expression of shock on his face. His touch seduced her but, his hands now rested in his lap, she wasn't under his spell. She had to trust him, to tell him. It was now or never.

"We can't stay here. I can't stay here Joel." She was torn. She couldn't leave him and had to tell him everything, including the creepy feeling that there was something inside the cabin she needed. Collecting all her willpower, the words sprayed from her mouth, "Since being here, I feel something. The violet light crawls inside me and forces urges I can't control. It speaks to me at a molecular level. Right now, it's telling me to tear this cabin apart."

The shock on his face turned to a scowl. Obviously, he didn't want to think about the reason he'd brought her to Wolf Manor. Maybe Caly and Miranda were right and he was attracted to her. "I think Selenia hid something here for me. Help me find it."

"Wow! You switch gears quick." The scowl on his face disappeared.

"I have a destiny that aches in every atom of my being. There's something in this cabin. It's why you brought me here."

His eyes dropped. "I was never told all the details. My job was to protect a growing girl who, for whatever reason, is important to the existence of humanity. I didn't expect to fall in love with her and now I can't imagine putting her into danger."

He said fall in love. She was definitely the *her* in his words. She didn't know what to do with it. *Should I admit my feelings for him? Are they obvious?* Now wasn't the time. She jumped up onto both feet. She finally got it -- it was all about protection, but she had a destiny that he couldn't protect her from. "The wolves can't hide me forever. Every bond that holds my body together is going crazy. I'm meant for a greater destiny, one that involves the crazy violet light that I can't escape. And something is in the cabin, something I need. You can help me find it or leave, but I'm going to find it." The words rolled off her tongue with haste.

His head drooped and he peered at her from under his thick, dark waves. "Violet light?"

"It's everywhere. You don't see it?" she asked, surprised, since she figured they did as they'd lined the blinds in the house. She assumed this was to hide it from her.

He didn't pursue a conversation about the light, instead he asked, "So where do we start?"

"Everywhere. We tear this place apart."

They checked every closet, beneath furniture and drawers, light fixtures, the bed, under sinks, everywhere in plain sight and hidden sight.

"Do you even know what we're looking for?" Joel asked, setting the mattress back onto the box springs. He raked his hand through his hair.

Mandy stood in the small closet. "No, but I'll know it when I see it." As she said it her eyes drifted to the ceiling. A door large enough for a small woman to fit inside with a short rope hanging from it was above her. "Aha!" she proclaimed.

Joel joined her. Their eyes shifted from the door to each other. He didn't waste time and pulled it down. A set of ladder steps folded down and Mandy scrambled up them. When she got to the top, she felt for a light switch and found another rope dangling above her head. She pulled it and a bright light blasted her eyes, making her blink as they adjusted.

The Monster Upstairs, Bloodseekers 2

An empty attic. The length of the cabin, separated by the vaulted ceiling, spanned before her. It was only about three feet high with a tiny crawl space beside the lift in the ceiling, giving her enough room. Several beams going both directions supported the house, insulation lay beneath them.

Carefully, she crawled across the beams, exploring the space. And feeling along everything solid. Even though chilly, sweat dripped down her forehead, stinging her eyes. She let go of a beam long enough to lift her shirt and wipe the sweat from them. When she did, she lost her balance, her foot going through the insulation.

She caught herself before plowing through the floorboards beneath it and thanked all her years of volleyball and the agility she'd learned. Her foot pushed enough insulation back it uncovered a small book. Her eyes lit up as she reached for it, being careful to plant her legs onto two vertical beams and lower her chest. She didn't want to crash through.

Once she grasped it, she slowly drew her hand back and, with care, tucked it into her waistband then turned herself around. The worn leather cover was soft against her abdomen. She spotted Joel's head through the opening as he watched with concern.

When she got closer, she saw his eyes shift to the book she'd tucked into her waistband. He climbed down the ladder and placed his hands around her waist as she climbed down, guiding each of her steps.

"What did you find?" he asked, dropping his arms to his sides.

She pulled out the book. "This."

"A book?"

Chapter 12

Alison and the Slayers

The Slayers met with Cody every day after school as he taught them to draw on their inner magic. Lacey and Alison had fewer problems because they each had their amulets, giving them an edge. Adrian and Rodham had more difficulty and Cody spent more time with them.

Rodham gained some of his telepathic abilities, but minimal. He had to concentrate and allow his mind to search out and grasp the energy of other minds. Once connected, his mind pried into theirs and he could send messages -- not exactly communication, but he could sway their thoughts and plant ideas in their heads.

Adrian gained the ability to transport objects, but not people. The secret they all learned was relaxing their physical bodies and allowing the energy "magic" inside them to rise to the surface. Once there, it did what they commanded it to.

Cody did a locater spell and found the missing amulets. As suspected, they were in the tunnels beneath Jacksonville. Alison gathered her strength as the group of five stood at the entrance to the tunnels. A brick rounded frame met the ground and chunks of cement and rubble littered the entrance.

She'd have to scoot on her belly in order to get inside.

Lacey twisted her mouth sideways. "Can you fit?"

Alison lifted a brow. "Not easily, can you open it up a bit more?"

Lacey nodded and raised her arms. She wiggled her fingers and chunks of cement lifted off the ground and were transplanted away from the entrance. "Better?"

She'd still have to scoot, but at least she'd be able to see what she was scooting into instead of heading in there blind. "Thanks."

Lacey's lips curved into a smile of satisfaction.

Their plan was for Cody, Lacey, Rodham, and Adrian to hold hands in order to funnel and strengthen their magic, giving Lacey the strength to pull the water in the tunnels back and hold it, Adrian the strength to teleport their amulets and maybe Veronica if Alison found her, and Rodham the ability to connect with Alison's thoughts as she traipsed through the tunnels alone.

Alison swallowed as she turned from the group and took her first step towards the rubbly entrance. She squatted and sat on her butt, legs dangling into the dark beyond. The brick facing was no more than an inch above her head. She gripped the dirt and dropped down as slowly as possible, but the dirt trickled through her fingers and she skidded to the ground, stumbled, and landed on her butt on the wet, muddied cement.

"Are you OK?" came Rodham's voice on loudspeaker in her mind.

She stood and instinctively dusted herself off, spreading the mud across her butt. "Yeah, I'm fine."

"What do you see?"

"A brick tunnel." She twisted around to get her bearings. "Some type of pipe runs across the roof." Her eyes followed it. "Round globes are attached to it. Lights maybe." She carefully walked closer to the first one and inspected it with her eyes. "Yup, lights."

She also noted that cracks ran across the tunnel's ceiling, which didn't give her a sense of security. Swirls of mud covered the ground, with a few wet patches of cement in between. It smelled earthy and musty, like mildew, but it didn't smell like Bloodseeker pheromones. She lifted her shirt over her nose and progressed forward using the light of her amulet to guide her way.

She wasn't alone, as Rodham stayed with her in thought and Cody fed her a mental map. The red glow gave the tunnel a dreamlike appearance, as if she was a character in one of the many books she'd read.

Fear gripped her as she made the first turn, and the realization she was moving further away from the Slayers and safety. Her legs grew shaky as nothing but empty tunnel spanned before her. *Get a grip!*

She willed her legs to move forward and took in her surroundings with every step.

Talk to me, Rodham urged.

Mind-talking with Rodham occupied her mind, made her forget the loneliness and fear that riveted her insides. She didn't even notice the shadow that lurked around the next bend. *It's all brick, except the ceiling looks like concrete blocks patched together. Some bricks have cracked and chipped over time but it looks solid. I guess it won't crash on me.*

We wouldn't let that happen.

They wouldn't under normal circumstances, but under the current ones it didn't seem likely a lifesaving rescue was on the menu. Lacey's power was tied up and Rodham and Adrian's were limited. Cody; she didn't know exactly how strong he was. She shook the depressing thoughts from her head and wrapped her arms around her middle as a cool breeze swept over her. A visible shudder surged over her small frame and every hair on her body prickled in unison.

She sucked in a deep breath, getting a mouthful of T-shirt. The whole idea was hers, not anyone else's, and she had to come through. Take one for the team. Drinking in the eeriness of the tunnel, she continued forward, trying to occupy her mind with pleasant thoughts of Rodham.

At first, she'd hated that he could read her mind and that she no longer had private thoughts. Most of those thoughts included Rodham, so was really embarrassing. After the last couple weeks, since his amulet was stolen, she'd missed the constant mind chatter and private conversations they had. Communicating now wasn't quite the same, he couldn't directly read her mind unless she projected the thought his way.

Tiny steps skittered across the floor in front of her. She halted, her heart thumping against her chest, and she projected her light towards the noise. Several rats scurried across the tunnel floor. She opened her mouth to scream, her shirt dropped, and she quickly clamped her hands over her mouth. To be invisible meant no sound either.

She gritted her teeth and continued on after the rats were gone. She rounded another corner and a small green glow emanated from further into the tunnel, right before the next bend. The mental map Cody fed her had both amulets much further in, but she didn't put it past the witch to move them around from time to time. She had to know the Slayers would be searching for them and Veronica.

Her heart skipped, the green glow from the amulet was only a few paces ahead. She ran towards it, then stopped and slowed, reminding herself not to blow her invisibility with noise. Her pulse raced with excitement as the light grew larger and brighter the nearer she got. This was easier than she thought, and relief washed over her at the idea of getting out of the creepy tunnel sooner.

She scurried towards it, Rodham's amulet, forgetting the rotten stench and how obnoxiously nasty the tunnel was. Her light danced off the brick walls like a candle, but the green light glowed steady. She assumed because she was moving and it was sitting in one place.

A dark shadow passed through, blocking its light for a second. The hairs on her body prickled again as she halted. Clamping a hand over her chest, she stood as still as a mannequin, but nothing happened and the dark shadow was gone. She shrugged it off as her mind playing tricks on her.

When she reached the amulet, she studied it. Its silver chain hung from a crack in the ceiling as if by magic. *Duh, of course it's magic,* she told herself to ease her mind. The light bathed her as she jumped into the air, her hand grazing the amulet. An energy she didn't recognize buzzed through her fingers. The energy shot through her arm and down her body, causing her to crumple.

She collapsed to the tunnel floor onto her hands and knees. Within seconds, she shook it off. The feeling was like a shock of electricity, not the warm radiating energy of their amulets. She had never touched his amulet, only the silver chain, but expected the same caressing glow as hers.

Gross! She pushed herself up and wiped her wet hands on her jeans, leaving a matching trail of muck above her knee caps. The tunnel was empty, void of anything she could use as a step stool. *I found yours, but can't reach it.*

After a few seconds, he responded. *Send a mental picture so Adrian can teleport it.*

That's so simple, why hadn't I thought of it? she mumbled inside her head.

Because you have me.

Holy crap! You can hear my thoughts!

You projected that one. I can't hear them all yet, but can't wait for that mental picture so I can start prying into your beautiful, dirty mind again.

OMG! She shook her head. *You're such a guy.* She chuckled inside. His silly comment lessened her trepidation.

She concentrated on the path she followed, the exact path Cody fed her mind, then stared at the amulet. Closing her eyes, she sent the picture the same way she communicated with Rodham.

Within seconds the amulet's chain wiggled. The stone swayed as it loosened from the ceiling. She stepped backwards as dirt and small chunks of ceiling loosened with the amulet. Her eyes scanned the roof and she stood in a running stance in case the whole tunnel collapsed and she needed to get out quick.

That's not it, came an anxious voice -- not Rodham's. She jumped in panic, then relaxed as she realized the voice was Cody's.

The amulet dangled by its clasp. *I'm looking at it. It's green, glowing, looks like it belongs to my large green elf. What are you talking about?*

I heard that, replied Rodham with a mind chuckle.

According to my spell it's further into the tunnel. Adrian stopped the movement. Get out of there now! Cody urged.

What the heck! she shouted mentally, as the thought of staying in the rank tunnel longer filled her.

Keep going. Witches, especially night witches, are tricky.

I hate these blasted, annoying night, dark whatever they are witches! She blew out a large sigh and stepped forward, the dangling amulet fell from the ceiling as she passed beneath it. Before it hit the ground she was knocked forward with enough force it sent her skidding on her stomach against the moist floor. The old transportation rails not visible beneath the mud sent sharp pains through her ribcage.

A loud grinding filled her ears and something crashed to the floor behind her, the vibrations shaking the stone and rails beneath her belly. She turned her head in time to see a set of large blades like a massive bear trap dropping from the roof and grating against the floor. Instinctively she curled her legs towards her chest.

Holy moly! She scrambled to her feet to run forward but another set of large blades dropped where she almost stood. Alison brought her hand to her heart and turned in the other direction when another set dropped, even closer this time. She twisted right, then left, searching for a direction to run. More grinding sent waves of sharp pain through her eardrums as another set dropped, leaving no more than six inches of clearance.

"Over here," said a voice with a thick British accent. "Skivvy up. There isn't all day for you to make up your mind."

She found the voice. It was attached to an odd looking creature with wild brown hair, a large nose, and round cheeks peering at her with two outstretched hands from a hole in the bricks no more than a foot or so above her head. Another set of blades hit the ground and she jumped, reaching for the creature's hands. He grasped them and pulled her upward while she planted her feet along the wall and climbed it.

"'Bout time. Follow me," he said as he crawled through the small space. It was large enough for him to crawl, as he was no larger than a four-year-old child. She felt like a giant and had to wriggle on her belly, her ribs throbbing with each movement, and the dampness soaking through her shirt and jeans. She was glad she wore old clothes and running shoes for her little venture. The gunk coating the crawl space oozed through her fingers as she clutched between the bricks to get to the other side.

What's happening? demanded Rodham.

It was a booby trap. I'm OK.

The creature jumped out of the space and grabbed her hands, pulling her out. She was impressed with his strength as she tumbled out of the tunnel onto her butt and the gunky ground of yet another tunnel. He was no more than half her height and she wasn't exactly tall at five foot three inches.

"Thank you," she said, lifting her aching body off the ground. She felt like an old woman and desired a long, hot bath filled with bubbles and the scent of strawberry or vanilla, anything but the nasty odor that coated every inch of her body and made her cringe.

"It's not every day I find a young lass traveling these tunnels," he muttered. "Or anyone..." he finished, his voice trailing off.

"I'm Alison."

"Alistair," he replied, but it sounded more like Alister. "Better get along then," he said, walking away from her.

He can't go, she thought and chased after him, the pain in her side smarting with each step. "Wait."

He stopped mid-step and waited. She caught up to him. "You save my life and leave. You know these tunnels well?"

He nodded. His wild hair appeared as flames, shaking with the movement of his head. It dawned on her that he could see her. Even though shook up, she hadn't felt a change in her energy status.

"You see me?" she asked with uncertainty.

"Ah, that I do. And you see me."

She wasn't in the mood for riddles. *What did he mean?* It didn't matter. Right now, all that mattered was finding those amulets. The real ones and, hopefully, Veronica. "I'm looking for something. Can you help me?"

"Depends on what yer looking for," he said, his eyes narrowed.

"Two amulets. They glow like me, but one is green, the other indigo."

He scratched his head then pulled his chin. "Seeing the place has traps, I expect a payment."

She doubted US dollars meant anything to the creature. "We can work a deal. What can I do for you?" She beamed, ready to do just about anything to get out of the nasty tunnels and home.

His eyes enlarged and he shot a smile missing a couple front teeth.

Chapter 13

Mandy

Joel slept on the couch. His long body spread across the length of it and his arm draped over the seat resting on Mandy's shoulder. The fire dwindled as she sat crossed legged with her back against the couch on the fur rug in front of it.

She was so taken by reading, she couldn't put the book down. The inscription on the first page said: *If you can read this, you are a Slayer.* Immediately, her attention was drawn to it. To Joel's eyes it was blank. On the outside it was a plain leather journal, worn soft with age. Inside, the pages were yellowed at the edges.

She turned one after the other and read about the battle between Bloodseekers and witches. A nasty sorceress centuries ago was so vain she couldn't accept death, instead she fought death by making herself the first Bloodseeker. She continued creating more Bloodseekers. Mandy guessed immortality wasn't what she cracked it up to be. The creatures lived off the blood of others. The witches of the night were her helpers.

They became so many in number that an organization of witches of the light came together and spelled seven amulets, one for each color of visible light. The group of seven individuals, all in the witches' bloodlines, were sent to seek their amulets and use them to destroy Bloodseekers. These seven were called Slayers. Their amulets would pass to a descendant every other generation.

She'd always believed in the supernatural, but never had any proof it existed. Besides what she'd seen with her own eyes, she had a journal, only visible to her and other Slayers.

Each Slayer had a journal in which they wrote their adventures and anything they learned about their powers and killing Bloodseekers. The journal in her hands belonged to the amethyst Slayer. There was no doubt in her mind it belonged to her and Carlito knew it. She was the strongest of all the Slayers and had the power to heal people. She thought of her mom and the surge of power that streamed from somewhere inside her, giving her mother a few more seconds of life. If only she'd had the amulet then.

Pushing her thoughts to the back of her mind, she continued reading. The Slayers were strongest in number and when all seven came together they could destroy all Bloodseekers on Earth by holding hands. Their lights combined and gave a stunning blaze that turned the Bloodseekers to ash.

She skipped ahead, scanning for something that gave her a clue why the werewolves found her so valuable. And she found it. She lifted her knees and propped the book on her legs. Joel quietly snored behind her. The fire was nearly gone and the cold air settled around her but she was so engrossed she didn't notice.

The Monster Upstairs, Bloodseekers 2

The date *February 29, 2000* she recognized immediately as it was her birthday.

Malina, a light witch and my grandniece was found wandering outside Wolf Manor, but she wasn't alone. With her were her boyfriend, an estranged night witch, and their child in her womb. The light witches forced her to leave and bound her powers. Her boyfriend managed to sneak away from the night witches, but not without penalty. His powers were also bound and he was forever marked. If found, he'd be killed. With nowhere to go they came to the werewolves because of my ties.

Something Joel said niggled at a corner of her brain, but she couldn't quite grab hold of it. She continued reading.

I couldn't leave her, with a baby in her womb, to die at the hands of others. I knew the night witches would hunt for both of them, but I couldn't endanger the wolves who'd always shown me kindness and generosity. So I called in a few light witches to place wards around their land, hiding it from the eyes of others. They didn't approve of the situation, but vowed not to let the word out as to where my vanquished grandniece was located.

The baby was too precious and special. She was the future amethyst Slayer and would one day take my place. I write this with a heavy heart, and I'm truly sorry that we did this, but there was no other way to protect you and you are far too important for humanity. Topaz, the seer Slayer, knows the truth as I couldn't hide the future from one who sees it. You and your sister have the combined strength to heal the path of the broken and set them free.

The sudden change from first to second person now made the message personal. Before, it was more like reading a great book. The reality of her situation sunk in as she read further. The words coming alive in her mind.

The baby was born, but not the one we expected. A twin who will one day be a very strong witch. Two hours later, you were born.

A twin, I have a twin! So many times she'd felt something, a tug at her heart she couldn't explain and phantom pains. The other half to her whole. So much of her life that she accepted as normal and assumed everyone else did too came rushing at her. *Where is my sister? Are we identical? Will I recognize her?* She had to get to her. An ache scrambled up her spine and settled in her stomach as it flip-flopped. Her sister was in trouble and she needed to find her!

She shook her head to rid the eerie feeling and continued reading.

The amulet bathed you in a purple haze and I knew beyond any doubt you were my successor. To protect you, we sent you away to live with the werewolf who found your parents in the woods and her son. We sent your twin to live with a family of Shiftlings in St. Augustine.

The niggling came front and center. Her great aunt saved Carlito but wasn't able to save Joel's father. He said they were Slayers. *That's why they're so darned protective of me! Holy moly! My sister's in St. Augustine -- in trouble. They think they're hiding the amulet from me but, if it's true, lead alone can't block gamma rays — amethyst -- violet light. The strongest of all Slayers.* Placing her thumb on the current page, she flipped backwards. She ran her fingers over the page, scanning for the words until she found them. *Garnet red Slayer has the power of invisibility, Agate orange is empathic, Emerald green is telepathic, Beryl yellow is telekinetic, Topaz blue can see the future, Onyx indigo is a teleporter, and Violet Amethyst is a healer, the strongest of the Slayers. Red is the weakest.* Her brain raced as she finished reading the final couple sentences entered in the journal.

Your parents were sent away to live human lives and asked to never return, nor would they ever find the place again as the wards are strong and they are powerless.

I'm waiting in the tower for you.

Mandy's eyes widened as she read the last words. The tower, the glow, they called to her, but how did she get into the tower. She'd tried already. She flipped through the rest of the pages but they were empty.

She dropped the book onto the floor and climbed on the couch beside Joel. He looked too peaceful to wake. She'd tell him in the morning. There was no one else, and he'd given up his life to protect her. He wouldn't hurt her.

Her heavy eyelids dropped and dreams of supernatural creatures and battles filled her mind.

Chapter 14

Alison and the Slayers

It turned out Alistair was a boggart who came to America centuries ago -- which explained how they were able to see each other. Her high level energy status that made her invisible to everyone put her in the spirit realm. It also explained the strange shadows and cool air she'd felt exploring the tunnels earlier.

To her luck, it turned out he didn't like the Evil One, as he called her, that used the tunnels as a hiding place for no good. She assumed he meant the night witch, but didn't bother to correct him. She was happy to have him on her side. For the past couple weeks he'd been haunting her, so to speak, by making her life as horrible as he could. He'd misplaced objects she left there and made a mess of the area she used. Upset when she returned to find her stuff discombobulated, she placed wards around the area and they successfully kept him out.

Unfortunately, she had wards around the amulets as well. They struck a deal -- she had to make the witch disappear and he'd take her to the amulets. She agreed that she and the other Slayers would find a way to get her out of the tunnels for good, but she needed the amulets to make it happen and a couple light witches more powerful than her.

She kept the light witch part to herself, as she needed him. He agreed.

He also confirmed she had someone trapped further in the tunnels in an area she kept highly guarded by creatures with glowing eyes, sharp fangs, and who stank of iron and death. Alison recognized the description and hoped she wouldn't be seeing or battling any for a while, but she was wrong. They'd have to face the Bloodseekers again and soon. Alistair slipped past them with ease, since they couldn't see into the spirit world, but her wards around the individual blocked him and the creatures from getting to her.

The glow of the amulets bathed her in warmth, bringing her out of her thoughts. Their colors intermingled in streaks of emerald, onyx, and topaz. *Topaz!* They hadn't met the topaz Slayer yet -- how did she get the amulet? Then she remembered how they found Rodham's inside the Bloodseekers' apartment.

After cutting a deal with Alistair, she notified the Slayers and Cody. Without much choice, they all agreed to help. Cody was the only one with no stake in it, yet he wanted to help. She was sure he had motivation other than the kindness of his heart, but she didn't have a single clue what it might be.

Cody gave her instructions to chant *Dame fuerza, la luz oscura se debilita* and push her hands in the direction of the amulets. He'd channel his magic through her. She didn't know what it meant, or even what language it was, but had no alternative than to do it. He said it'd give her five minutes to go in, grab them, and get out. *Once you have them, run like the boogie man is chasing you towards the entrance,* he said.

She sucked in a deep breath while Cody counted to three, then she chanted with arms stretched in the direction of the amulets. A surge of power struck her body, forcing her to stumble forward. It streamed from her fingertips and the air surrounding the amulets crackled. *Now Alison!*

She ran forward and grabbed all three amulets in one movement, then hurdled forward and shot through the tunnels, forgetting the aches and sharp pain in her ribs, Alistair at her side. *On my way!* she shouted mentally at Rodham. A rumble echoed through the tunnels and she felt heat against her back but didn't look. She continued forward until she saw the light from the outside shining through the gap. She grabbed the dirt and scrambled up the side, hoisting herself out of the mouth. Rodham caught her arm and pulled her upwards and out of the tunnel.

A giant ball of fire rushed at her, seen with her peripheral vision, and nearly singed her arm as she reached down and grabbed Alistair's hand, pulling him onto the platform. A rush of water washed over the fireball and his legs.

Laying on the dirt and rubble, breathing heavily, she looked up at familiar faces and dropped the amulets on the ground beside her. All eyes stared at the brilliant topaz light meant for the next Slayer with the ability to see the future.

Chapter 15

Mandy

Mandy awoke to Joel lying beside her, his hand smoothing her hair. Morning light streamed through the curtain and bathed the room. Heat radiated from him and his muscles bulged against her from their proximity.

"Good morning," he said in a gentle voice.

"Hey." Then her discoveries from the journal ran at high speed through her head and her eyes widened. "We need to go."

He lifted a brow. "Now?"

"Yes." She wiggled beneath him and he lifted up, sitting on the edge of the couch. "Carlito is hiding something. I don't know why, maybe I do, and I don't think he's left Wolf Manor at all." Thoughts that manifested in her sleep came to her conscious mind.

He narrowed his eyes at the mention of Carlito. "Why would he lie?"

She stood. "My great aunt saved his life, but was too late to save your father. Every curtain in that house is lined with lead, but lead won't keep out gamma rays -- the strange violet light I see everywhere. I didn't tell you this, but my first night I went upstairs, following an urge, and saw Carlito leaving a hidden room in the tower."

He stared at her with vacant eyes. "You're not making any sense."

"Of course not, you can't read the book." She picked the book up from the floor, feeling something in the back. She flipped to it and noticed the binding was loosened. She stuck her finger inside and wiggled it. Her finger touched a plastic card inside. Wriggling it, and hanging the book at an angle, she managed to get it beneath her finger and slowly pulled it out. Turning it around in her hand, she realized it was a keycard. Her face lit up. *It opens the door!*

"We need to get to the tower now. I have to save my sister!" With that she stomped towards the door and ran into the near-freezing morning air. She'd run the entire way to the house if she needed to. He didn't have to believe her or back her. Well aware she probably sounded like a mad woman crazed by demons, she didn't care. This was her mission. The destiny she was born to uphold.

As her thought finished, she felt something soft nuzzle her hand. She glanced and Joel trotted beside her and nuzzled her hand again motioning for her to jump on. Mid-sprint she grabbed hold of him and threw her body onto his back, again thankful for her past volleyball experience and general sports training. However in shape her body was, she was grateful she didn't have to run all the way to the mansion, and even more thankful he supported her whether he actually believed her or not. She'd prove it to him.

Joel slowed and climbed the steps of Wolf Manor then stopped. She kissed the top of his head then whispered, "Thank you," in his ear.

Mandy slipped off his back and opened the door. Joel nodded and followed behind her as they entered the large house. He trotted behind her as she stalked up the stairs and into his room where he changed into his human form and pulled on a pair of sweatpants. She'd grown used to watching him shift into and out of wolf form, but was still amazed and didn't understand how it didn't hurt. It looked horribly painful but he'd chuckled when she mentioned it and said, 'It doesn't hurt any more than wiggling your fingers.'

He strolled alongside her and grasped her hand, their gazes meeting as she squeezed his hand. No words exchanged, she walked alongside him.

The wolves in the house were beginning to stir, and smells of bacon, eggs, and coffee entered her nostrils. They flared as her stomach grumbled.

Caly bounced down the stairs, a toothy smile on her face. "Good morning!"

Mandy and Joel nodded with solemn faces, catching Caly off guard. She halted and grabbed Mandy's arm. "What's wrong?"

Mandy pasted on a fake smile. "Nothing. We'll be down for breakfast soon."

She dropped her arm to her side and narrowed her eyes then smiled and continued down the stairs.

They stood in front of the bloor and Mandy stared at the sliver in the wall, searching for a spot for the key card. Not finding one, she slipped the card into the sliver and swiped -- nothing. She twisted her mouth and turned on her heels, scanning the walls. A tiny red light blinked from the other side of the room. She hadn't noticed it before. It didn't matter. She marched to it and swiped the card across it.

The door opened and Joel's eyes grew wide as his gaze shifted from her to the door. She ran over and allowed the warm violet light to soak into her body.

"You're glowing," said Joel, a notch above a whisper.

She looked down at her legs and feet. The violet light enveloped her. She wasn't as bright as the light, but she'd light up a dark room enough to see more than shadows. She reached for his arm and they ran up the stairs together.

"Please sit," ordered Carlito as they entered the room, pointing towards two cream velvet chairs. Mandy's eyes widened. She knew he hadn't left, but was shocked to see him sitting calmly in a plush leather chair, an Asian screen with painted pink blossoms behind him. The glow radiating brightly everywhere in the room. It didn't appear to have a start or end.

Mandy's eyes searched the room for the glow. "Where is it?!" she demanded, taking a step towards him.

Carlito folded his hands beneath his chin. "Dear Mandy, you are a patient girl. I know all this is a lot to soak in, but you haven't once complained or demanded anything."

The Monster Upstairs, Bloodseekers 2

The anger burned in her eyes -- he could only be acting facetious. Either way, she didn't care. The light was hers and she was taking it!

Unfazed by her, he leaned back and set his hands in his lap. "Sixteen years ago we found a comrade, an ally outside the gates. It was Selenia, your mother who found her. With her was a man who was anything but an ally. Hmm... Keep your friends close and your enemies closer, as the saying goes. He was a witch of the night with the power to wield elemental magic and she a witch of the light with the power to wield light, read minds, and telekinesis. We brought them in as she was obviously with child."

Mandy pursed her lips. She didn't want to hear him out, but knew she couldn't take him. He was far stronger than her. Anger boiled inside her as she listened.

He drew in a deep breath. "As wolves, we stay out of business not our own, but this witch's great aunt was a powerful and kind ally. She saved many a wolf's life with the touch of her hands and she kept us secret. We had no choice. Out of good conscience we couldn't turn them and the baby away. Yes, being the grandniece, we all knew that meant the baby could bear the gene, could be the one. We got far more than we bargained for."

Mandy sat still, squeezing Joel's hand as she listened to the story.

"There are very dark forces on this Earth, created by a vain sorceress. Legend calls them vampires. We call them Bloodseekers. The night witches are the sorcerous blood kin, but witches can be fickle creatures. Where there is a malevolent evil, there is a benevolent good. In light of that, the Slayers were born, created by witches of the light. There are seven in total. You, my dear, are the strongest -- the amethyst Slayer. When you bond with the amulet, the power will transfer to you."

Mandy blinked her eyes rapidly. "I know this already. Tell me something I don't know," she said with her clenched mouth.

He nodded, his face solemn. "Yes, there's more. You weren't born alone, you have a twin."

"I know!" She stood, hands on her hips.

"Sit, dear. You heard me. She was born first. Let me backtrack. When we brought them onto the grounds, your great aunt put the amulet towards your mother's belly and it glowed brighter than ever and swung towards her. We knew you were in there, but when labor came and the baby was born the amulet didn't glow for her. An hour later you entered the world, after midnight on leap day. The amulet glowed bright as a newborn star, nearly blinding everyone, and you lit up like a bulb. Your great aunt was surrounded by a halo of light. You see, it made sense that you were a twin. Your parents were of opposing forces, and where there is light, there is dark."

Mandy sat on the edge of one of the chairs and stared at Carlito, her mouth agape. After several seconds of silence she mouthed, "Are you saying my sister is evil?!"

He chuckled. "Not exactly. Yes, you are the light but she, like you, was brought up in a similar situation. Within the past couple years her powers have shown themselves and she fights alongside the Slayers. She can wield the elements as well as the light. Her powers are a combination of the light and the dark and her soul is good. We believe the two of you, united, have powers that can cure the dark."

"Where is she?" she demanded. Even as the words left her mouth she knew the answer, but she wanted to hear him admit it.

His mouth formed a straight line. "She was taken."

She fell back in the cream velvet chair. Yes, her instinct was right. She had to save her sister. "I need the amulet to save her!"

A beautiful, small-framed woman came around the Asian screen, entering the room. Her straight hair dark, and glowing violet, almond-shaped eyes. The light bathed her body, emanating from an amethyst stone hung around her neck by a delicate silver chain. She spoke in a soft voice as she lifted the chain from her neck. "Mandy," her thin lips pulled back in a smile, "it's a pleasure to meet you."

With the amulet dangling from her left hand, she used her right to reach for Mandy's hand, then placed the silver chain of the amulet on Mandy's palm and she wrapped her fingers around it. "It's time for you to take this. I've worn it long enough. Your sister needs you."

Mandy stared at her, then the amulet. The source of violet light dangling from her fingertips. She'd yearned for it and now was speechless.

The woman leaned close to Mandy and folded her arms around her. She returned the hug. The tiny woman pulled away. "Go, but don't put the amulet around your neck just yet. You'll need the bonding power to ash the Bloodseekers who guard your sister."

Mandy opened her mouth, then closed it. Small lines webbed across the woman's face. She blinked, thinking it a trick of the light, or her mind playing games, but it wasn't. She was aging in front of her.

Joel spoke up. "You heard her. We need to go."

"I'm going too," said a female voice. Mandy turned. Calypso and Miranda stood in the doorway.

Carlito, who'd sat quietly, now stood and wrapped his arm around the tiny woman -- her great aunt. He held her lovingly and she understood why he prolonged it. He was in love and she was aging rapidly since taking the amulet from around her neck.

"I'm sorry, Carlito," Mandy said as a small tear dropped from the corner of her eye.

"Go. This is your birthright, and your twin's life is in danger," Carlito replied in a soft but firm voice.

She grabbed Joel's hand then glanced at the sister wolves who looked at her apprehensively but ready to take on the world.

Chapter 16

Alison and the Slayers

They decided to take turns protecting the topaz amulet and to Alison's dismay she drew the short stick and had it the first week. Alistair was an unlikely ally she sorely needed, but the idea of killing the witch turned her stomach inside out. The Bloodseekers weren't even close to human, not in her book anyways, with their gnarled fingers and dagger-like teeth protruding from their gums.

A promise was a promise. Alistair had helped them and they'd help him. When they departed, he went back into the tunnels. As a spirit, he didn't need air to breath so the water had no impact on him. He'd alert them and they'd fulfill their promise, although she truly wanted only to save Veronica.

Her mind returned to the witch. She'd never got a good look at her face, but from the glimpses she'd taken the witch reminded her of someone, but she couldn't place who. Her hair a flaxen silver with bright violet eyes. It raked at her brain, and the more she thought about it, the more it irritated her that she couldn't place where she'd seen her before. Maybe she hadn't and was only imagining it.

She blew out a long breath, deciding to call her Gran. Her brain a murmur of thoughts. *How did the witch get the amulet? Where did she get it from? Who is or was… the topaz Slayer?*

She picked up her tablet and Skyped her Gran, sucking up the independent big girl act because she was curious yet a chicken and stressed, worried and upset. If she hadn't moved to Florida she'd still be oblivious to Bloodseekers and other strange creatures. She wasn't sure who she could or couldn't trust aside from the other Slayers. Cody was cool, but it was just too easy. He pops into their lives at the exact moment they need a light witch. He teaches them how to harness the magic inside them, yet what was in it for him?

Gran answered and Alison cringed at how old she had grown and so quickly. Her face a mass of wrinkles and her vibrant, thick red hair now mostly white and thinning. Dull amber eyes took the place of brilliant amber ones. She blinked rapidly to fight the tears festering behind her eyelids and pulled back her lips in a forced smile.

"Hi Gran," she said in a shaky voice.

"Ally, you don't have to be strong for me. My life's been full and I'll always be with you so long as you wear that amulet and journal your discoveries for the next Slayer," her voice cracked with age.

Her words triggered the waterfall and tears coursed down Alison's cheeks. Her Gran was right but, even so, she didn't want her to die. She was aging decades daily. "We… we found the… um… topaz amulet."

"Where Ally?"

She relayed finding Cody, and her tunnel beneath Jacksonville adventure, and didn't forget to mention Alistair. By the time she finished her tears had all but dried up.

"When topaz discovered his wife was ill with cancer, he made a choice to die with her and took off his amulet, locking it in a vault beneath Jacksonville. You see, many years ago, bankers used those vaults to store money. But with all the advances in technology it isn't necessary anymore and he couldn't think of a better place to hide it until his successor was of age to bond with it."

Alison's eyes teared up again after hearing about his choice to die with his wife. It saddened her, and she didn't understand why, if they have magical power, he didn't call on the amethyst Slayer to make his wife whole -- after all, wasn't that the amethyst power? She asked her Gran as much and she responded.

"We all have to pass. We can't live forever and I'm sure he was confident in his successor claiming the amulet in due time," she paused for a few seconds and the air became still. "Topaz and Amethyst were the best of friends for many, many years until… they had a falling out of sorts. It happened about sixteen, seventeen years ago. The rest of us weren't privy to what happened, and no matter what we always have each other's backs."

She rolled the idea in her head, kneading it and turning it over like bread dough. Something clung to her mind, but no matter how she worked it, she couldn't quite hold onto the idea so switched gears.

"What about Cody? He's nice, but I don't trust him… at least not completely."

Gran smiled, the wrinkles in her face forming deep grooves. "Always remember, witches have their own agenda but that doesn't mean he hasn't been watching you for a while and chose your moment of need to show himself."

She'd said it before, witches have their own agenda and she didn't doubt that he had one. Although, for the life of her, she couldn't figure it out. "That's what I was hoping to find out."

"I don't have all the answers you seek. We learn and write it down so the next Slayer can build on our discoveries. His parents both being light witches, his agenda could be anything from solid wanting to help you to a secret motivation steeped in centuries of drama," she took in a deep breath. "The first Slayers had nothing; empty journals, not even an amulet. They had to find them and paved the way for all of us since."

The thought hanging at the edge of her brain snaked its way into a full thought and she blurted it out, "We are witches! I mean we come from a light witch bloodline but we only have one power. Can we tap into other powers? And why isn't everyone in our bloodline a witch?"

Gran's eyes rounded like balls on her face. "Listen carefully, you are special. All the Slayers are special. The secret isn't tapping into the magic. The secret is learning to channel the magic into your amulets. Once you learn to do that, your special power will surpass that of any witch. As for our family having or not having magic I can only speculate."

Alison clung to her words.

"I think we are all born with magic, but only those who use it by a specific age become witches. For the rest," her face became stoic, "it stays in their genes, dormant, and passes on to their children. I asked myself that question when I was young, until I learned to stop asking the questions and pay attention to what I observed."

Chapter 17

Mandy

Mandy dropped the amulet into the front pocket of her jeans and a sudden jolt of electricity vibrated through her. It comforted her, yet made her feel fearless. She turned back and gave Carlito a death glare. "Taken by whom?" she demanded

He swallowed and leaned forward, resting his folded hands on the large desk. "The sorceress herself."

She dragged her hands over her face. "The mother of vampires? Why, how does everybody even know about us? I'm missing something, you're not being straight with me."

He rested his gaze on hers. "There are seven Slayers, right now four have banded together; garnet with the power of invisibility, emerald with the telepathy, beryl who uses telekinesis, and onyx the transporter. You make five. Topaz can see the future and predicted your birth. He saw it, telling your great aunt. In his vision, he didn't see your sister. It wasn't until sometime later he had another vision. In it he saw you and your sister binding your light together and Bloodseekers walking in your blinding light who were no longer Bloodseekers."

"Soo... where is this topaz Slayer?"

Joel, who'd sat quiet through the entire story, finally spoke. "After the vision, he took his amulet off and has since passed away. Nobody yet knows who the next Slayer is that will take his spot."

Everyone in the room stared at him with mouths agape. Finally the tiny woman spoke. "He passed several years ago. In the car waiting at the gate you will find his journal under the front seat. Mandy, you will be able to read it just as you do your own. When you find the next topaz Slayer, it is your duty to give him the journal."

Mandy straightened her back. "You have the journal but not the amulet?"

A warm, reminiscent smile crossed the tiny woman's face. "He was my best friend and an honest man. You will find everything you need inside his journal and, I'm sure, the location of the amulet." The woman's supple skin looked crepier every second.

Mandy nodded and turned to her werewolf cohorts. She walked between them, her head held high, and marched down the stairs and out the front door. Finally she was leaving and with the crazy violet light that begged her to find it.

They piled into the car. It wasn't any car, but a Cadillac Escalade, loaded with all the bells and whistles. Joel at the wheel, the gates opened and they pulled onto the road. She was no longer trapped but felt a military carrier load of sorrow for Carlito. She understood the heartbreak of losing someone and judging by the woman's rapid aging it wouldn't be long at all. Most likely more the reason for not sticking around than finding her sister. Her twin was her age and had a long life ahead of her, one she hoped they'd spend getting to know each other. The woman, her great-aunt, had weeks at the most to live.

She plugged St. Augustine into the GPS for guidance and felt below her seat until her fingers caressed the soft leather of the journal. She pulled it out and flipped through the pages until she found the last entry. She read. It was a freakin' poetic riddle. *What is it with riddles?*

Perturbed she read silently.

The First Coast large and bold but beneath lies the secret only you behold.

"What the—" she said aloud. Three sets of eyes on her. "Oops!"

"What is it?" offered Miranda.

She read it aloud.

"The first coast," mumbled Caly. Then her eyes lit up and she whipped out her phone. Everyone sat silent and after a few minutes she blurted, "Jacksonville, Florida is commonly called the First Coast. It's like a nickname and is just north of St. Augustine."

Joel piped in, "Only you behold. Only the proper Slayer can use the power of the amulet."

Mandy snickered. "Holy crap, we have to go beneath the city. So, how do we get there?"

Everyone was transfixed by the search engines on their phones except Joel. He kept his eyes on the road. Within twenty minutes they had a clear idea. They found two distinct sets of tunnels. One that was used for transportation in the past but now filled with water. The other used in the past by banks to store money. They agreed an old vault beneath the city would be the perfect place to hide something, and Mandy reset the coordinates to Jacksonville.

They made several pit stops along the way. Mandy took note of the chilly air that grew warmer and more humid with every stop. In the early morning hours, they reached the Georgia-Florida border and, too stubborn and wound tight to stop, they continued until they reached Jacksonville and settled for the first hotel they found.

None too early, they arose the following morning, ate, and explored the city, finding the tunnels. With tours going in and out they waited until sunset. It would be a long night, so they grabbed a bite and took a nap.

In the back of the Escalade they found duffle bags filled with clothes and money. The werewolves were resourceful and didn't leave anything uncovered. Mandy changed her clothes, tossing her old jeans into the duffle along with the amulet she'd stuffed into her front pocket. Without it, she felt weak and human. She sank her hand into her pocket and a rush of electricity seized her body.

"What is it?" asked Joel, running to her side.

She let go and stumbled backwards. "The amulet. I touched it. I'm not supposed to touch it yet," was all she squeaked out. *Will it do that again when I place it around my neck?* It was like the electricity was bonding with the energy in the chemical bonds that held her body together, becoming stronger.

Joel reached in her discarded jean pocket and pulled out the amulet. He then stuffed it into her fresh pants pocket. "How's that?" he asked with a crooked smile.

"Better." The gentle hum of electricity it caused returned to her. She wasn't ready yet for the full blast that would surely transform her in some way.

They'd changed hotels so they were within walking distance of the tunnels' entrance. The tunnels were located beneath Atlanta Bank and Sun Trust. Once underground, the wolves changed as they were more powerful and fierce in wolf form, should they run across a witch or something else with evil intentions. Their teeth also came in handy for cutting the wires needed to sneak in through the ventilation system.

The wolves' eyes saw through the darkness and Mandy used the violet glow emanating from her pocket. The area was finished off and even included a tiny restaurant. She leaned against the wall, hitting the switch behind her and the place lit up. "This can't be it. We have lights and everything. There has to be something else," Mandy said, barely audible, but the wolves' keen hearing picked up each word.

Miranda shrugged, "They ran tours all day. Makes sense."

Mandy'd never seen a wolf shrug and giggled. They split up to explore and found subterranean offices still in use. Mandy found vaults upon vaults, but all were open and empty -- so many she lost count. She stood inside a large one and went through each safety deposit box -- all empty.

Slamming its door, she sank to the ground. The vaults were thick metal but she'd still be able to see its glow.

Joel strode up next to her and sat on his haunches. "Don't be down. If it's here we'll find it."

"It's not here. I'd see it glowing. There has to be a part of this tunnel that's been blocked off," she said in a defeated voice, resting her head against his soft back. She smoothed his fur and gently fluffed it. He nuzzled her face.

Paws scampered into the vault, interrupting their moment. "Sorry," said Caly, her white fur shimmering in the glow of the violet light. "I think I found something you need to see."

Mandy slowly pulled onto her feet and she and Joel followed Caly into an office, then through a door into a storage facility. Werewolf nails were great for picking locks, it turned out. It looked as though it hadn't been tampered with since it was built. Several jugs with *Drinking Water* printed on them in red ink were stacked beside a wall opposite Miranda, who sat near a vent with the screen removed.

"Once we moved the water, we found this. The screen had been tampered with already so we pulled it off. Our nails make great screwdrivers too," she said, a large smile on her face.

Mandy slowly stepped towards it and kneeled down to peer inside. She didn't see a blue light, but could see far enough inside to tell the space was large enough for her to crawl inside. It curved only a few feet from their location.

She moved her head away from the tunnel, still sitting on her knees. "I'm going in."

Joel offered, "I'm going in first. It might be a trap."

"No Joel," Mandy's eyes traced his muscled werewolf form, "you won't fit."

"Me or Caly will fit," offered Miranda.

Mandy, Caly, and Miranda exchanged glances, then Caly offered, "I found it. I'm going first."

She placed one front paw inside the crawl space, then the other, then her back paws until all of her disappeared into it. Mandy followed and stayed close to Caly, her tail tickling her nose. The entire space was made of cement, like it was built to hide something. There was no light. At least in the larger bank tunnels there were lights and they worked. Inside here was black, but her violet light shone against the walls like a black light.

Two distinct sets of finger prints, Caly's paw prints excluded, were on the walls and floor in front of her. At least two other people knew about the tunnel. They turned the corner, then another. Mandy took in a large breath, beginning to feel claustrophobic. There was no ventilation and sweat beaded over her body. She stared at Caly in front of her and felt better and glad that she'd come with her.

They followed another bend and a small blue light radiated through the seams of what appeared to be a vault at the end of the crawl space. *That's it,* she thought, but didn't say anything until they reached it.

"This is it. Do you see a blue light?" Caly said, expectantly.

"I do, but I'm not sure. Its energy feels different to mine."

"Different how?" asked Caly.

"I can't explain it. It's not warm and fuzzy or invigorating like mine. It's like… prickly." She wiped sweat from her brow before it stung her eyes. "I don't get it, but we're here, so how do we open this vault?"

Caly's wolf lips curved upward. "I have great hearing and won't miss a click. Can you slide in front of me?"

Mandy looked at the tiny gap Caly made by lengthening her body and plastering it alongside the cement wall. Mandy scooted forward, Caly backward, and with a little adjusting they switched places. She wiped her hands on her dryish shirt, then rubbed them together and placed them on the combination dial, Caly guiding her.

It clicked open and the small space glowed bright blue mingled with the violet light tucked away inside her pocket. The ground rumbled beneath them. Caly and Mandy swapped glances. Mandy grabbed the silver chain of the amulet and, without words, they crawled as fast as they could back to the room where Joel and Miranda waited for them.

The rumbling came now in waves, and dirt poured around them. In the distance, Mandy heard Joel's voice, "Man. Man," his tone distressed. Then she heard nothing and felt only sand surrounding her body. In her hand, the chain was firmly wrapped around her fingers.

Chapter 18

"Man," she heard, along with scratching, then something soft brushed against her face. She blinked her eyes open and bits of sand fell into them, stinging and blurring her vision, but she made out Joel's wolf face, his brown snout inches from her nose. She scrunched her eyes closed and lifted her arms, wrapping them around Joel.

Room temperature water spilled across her face, washing away most of the sand. Mandy blinked her eyes several times until she could see straight. They still burned, but they'd be fine after a nice warm shower. "Where's Caly?" she asked, her voice quivering as she worried Caly didn't make it out.

"Over here," Caly called, shaking sand out of her fur.

Mandy relaxed when she heard her voice and ducked under the flying particles of sand. "Watch out!" she said, snickering, happy that Caly was OK.

"Sorry," she said, walking in her direction and nuzzling her face, pushing her to the floor. They tussled for a bit.

"We should go," suggested Joel.

Mandy and Caly adjusted themselves and followed Joel and Miranda out of the tunnels. The wolves shifted and dressed before moving up to street level. With the coast clear, they rushed back to the motel, all of them ready for a shower -- especially Mandy and Caly.

After a shower, Mandy walked outside the room for fresh air. She leaned her arms against the black metal fence and perched her chin onto her clasped hands. The pool water moved in gentle waves from the three foot waterfall at the end. Lights glowed beneath, giving it a relaxing quality. Red, yellow, orange, green, blue, and purple; all the colors of the rainbow like the Slayer group she so recently learned she was part of.

What are the others like? And would she get to her twin in time to save her? She glanced to the sky. Rainbow colors filled it as the sun dropped beneath the horizon.

"What are you looking at?"

She jumped. Seeing Joel she let out a sigh and turned around, her back against the fence. "You scared me." Taking note of his delicious smile she added, "The colors of the rainbow. I see them all, some brighter than others. Do you see them?"

He leaned on the fence beside her and glanced to the sky. "I do, but doubt I see them as bright as you."

"Do you think we'll find them in time?"

"I hope so. We have the amulet and we'll leave tomorrow following your eyes." He smiled while a short breeze whipped his curl into his eyes.

She jabbed him. "My eyes. O...K..."

Another breeze ruffled the fronds of the palms surrounding the pool and, in the water, the beautiful dark-haired woman's face appeared. The wind carried the message: *where are you?*

In Jacksonville, she responded in her head and the woman's face vanished as the tiny waves rippled across it.

Several hours later in bed, Mandy wrestled. A black goo, thick as tar, ran over her face and body. She panicked. "Joel," she called as she felt for his presence, but everything was covered in a thick, black goo. Her heart ran cold. *Where's Joel?* "What the..." She attempted to sit up but the goo stuck her in place.

"Man," she heard Joel calling but couldn't feel him. She couldn't move.

"You're awake. I wondered how long it would take, oh... only about five minutes," said an unfamiliar, garbled, female voice. It was close.

Help, she called with her mind -- an instinctive action she didn't understand. She didn't expect a response and was shocked when a female voice answered.

Stay calm. Where are you?

The voice wasn't the same as the other and it didn't make the hairs on her arm hackle, so she took a chance and responded. *In a hotel in Jacksonville.*

Are you alone?

She's nosy! thought Mandy.

Look cheecka, I heard that. Now answer my question so I can help you.

More concerned about her immediate threat she responded. *No I'm with wolves. One is lying next to me trapped in the same goop I am. There's two more in the room next to us.*

It's a glubble bubble. I'm going to try and reach the other wolves. The one next to you has a distinct brain signature. I'm hoping the others do too.

It this telekinetic 911 or something? Stay on the line and talk with me until we reach your location.

I'm going to ignore that, and we don't have much time so cut out the sarcasm!

"You found my stone. Pretty clever, huh? I placed a locater spell on it. It works like magic GPS," said the voice, exuding confidence. She still couldn't place where it was coming from.

I think I found them. What are their names?

Calypso and Miranda. Hurry, I'm running out of oxygen.

"You're kinda special you know… and really quiet," she poked Mandy's gooey leg until she moved it. "If you just give me the amulet I'll leave."

Through her peripheral vision she noted a shadow. Focusing her eyes, she made out a fuzzy form.

I got them, but you need to keep her busy.

Keep her busy, she could do that. "OK, I don't want it anyway, but it's in bed with me so you'll have to get this goo off me and Joel."

"The wolf, hah! Nasty beasts."

"I can't give it to you until you do," Mandy persisted.

"Fine," she said and the goo disappeared. A jolt of energy rushed through her and when she blinked she was no longer in the hotel. Instead she was in a dark, still place. It was silent and void of anything. She couldn't move or feel anything around her, like her brain was trapped in a vacuum.

"Finally! We don't have much time at all. She'll be back soon, and if I don't get you back you'll be trapped here with me. Part of you will anyways," said the voice. The same one in her head, only now she wasn't inside her head, or Mandy was trapped inside her head. The thought of whose brain they were trapped in made her head hurt.

Mandy's eyes adjusted to the darkness and saw the form of a female. She felt a jolt of electricity run through her with her touch. Mandy tried to speak, but no words came out.

"Wow! Two souls in one. Take this," a cold metal object the size of a bottle dropped into her hand and another jolt of electricity buzzed through her.

Suddenly, she was back in the motel. Mandy sucked in a deep breath and lifted up. The small object was cupped in her hand. Glaring at her was a young woman, fifteen or so. The light of the moon touched her silver hair, streaking it with golden shadows, and her eyes were an odd shade of blue-violet. She looked at Joel still surrounded in goo. "The wolf too!"

She rolled her blue-violet eyes and the goo around Joel disappeared. "The amulet," she ordered, placing her hand out in front of Mandy's chest.

She didn't have a clue what just happened, but figured Silver Hair was a witch. Mandy fumbled beneath her pillow as if searching for the amulet and stuffed the small metal bottle underneath it. She was bluffing and hoped it lasted long enough for her to think of something else. At that moment a growling white wolf leapt directly for the intruder, but she slipped out of her grasp and disappeared.

The room melted around Mandy and she bolted upright in bed. Growling from the far corner of the room grabbed her attention. The three wolves stood in attack mode, with heads lowered and jaws extended, circling the far corner of the room.

Silver Hair flickered in the corner, surrounded by the wolves. "Crap!" she shouted as Joel's jaws clamped on her dress. She vanished but he'd managed to get a mouthful of the blue cloth.

"Who the heck is she?!" asked Mandy, not so much to Joel and the sisters, but as a general question.

The wolves turned in unison. Joel dropped the cloth and ran towards her. "You're OK." His brown-golden wolf eyes scanned every inch of her.

"What happened?"

"You were attacked by a witch."

It turned out the goo and everything was in her head. It was her wrestling under the covers that woke Joel, followed by what he called an earthy-fire odor. His first action was to wake her up, but she was somewhere else and, no matter how much he called, she didn't respond. Caly and Miranda heard him calling and panicking, so came right over through the attached door.

The witch put her in some type of alternate reality. She trapped her inside her own mind. The idea that something existed powerful enough to get inside her head and trick her sent shivers prickling through her body. Each hair stood on end.

Caly and Miranda hadn't moved from the spot, as if guarding something precious. "We got something. Look," said Miranda, a smile on her face.

Mandy and Joel padded to the spot and stared at the floor; a drop of blood. "What do we do with it?" shrugged Mandy.

"We save it and have a light witch analyze it," said Miranda matter-of-factly, like everyone had a light witch in their pocket.

"Do you know any?" asked Mandy with a 'yeah right' voice.

"One or two," Miranda smiled, lifting her eyebrows. "Doesn't everyone?"

Then Mandy remembered the other voice. The one she knew was coming from her head. She ran towards the bed to see if the little bottle was there or if all that was part of the witch's trick. She threw the pillow and there, beneath it, was the tiny metal bottle. She wrapped her fingers around it.

"What about this?" she asked, uncurling her fingers in front of the wolves.

Miranda shifted, appearing as comfortable naked as clothed. She tilted her head as she studied it in the palm of Mandy's hand. "Where did you get that?"

"A voice inside my head brought me somewhere and handed me this. When she placed this in my hand the caress of her skin against mine caused an electric jolt to travel through my body, then she said something like 'Two souls in one'."

"Wolves and witches aren't generally friends, but we fight the same fight and their job, as well as ours, is to protect you, so I'm sure she'll help and maybe tell us what this thing is," responded Caly, looking Miranda in the eye as if talking only to her.

Chapter 19

They got on the road quickly and didn't waste any time packing up and leaving. The location of the witch they were on their way to see took them south of Jacksonville and St. Augustine. Joel stayed on 1-95 until they hit highway 1 and they followed that over the intercostal to the beach.

Never in her life had Mandy seen the ocean. She gawked in awe as they drove the coastal road and bits of ocean peeked between houses and foliage. She unrolled her window and inhaled the salty air. They finally stopped at a small shop along the beach called Magik Essence.

It was in a strip mall surrounded by a pizza place, a sandwich shop, and a couple surf stores. The blue sign above the door was shaped like a crescent moon with the words *Magik Essence* printed across it in swirly, yellow letters.

The bell rang when they entered the store and a customer with her hair pulled into a bun and skinny as a street pole stood at the counter. The woman behind the counter, a young lady with bobbed blonde hair, lifted her eyes and smiled as Miranda and Caly entered. They split up and perused the store until the customer exited, then they pulled together.

The lady with the bob strolled from around the counter. She carried herself with an air of confidence. She had fine features set in her heart-shaped face and full lips. "Miranda, Caly. It's been so long. How are your parents?"

She gave them each a hug and peck on the cheek.

"They're good," said Caly. "This is Joel and Mandy."

The lady brought her hands in front of her. "Nice to meet you. I'm Zoe."

Miranda sucked in her lips and shifted as if nervous. "We need some help."

She nodded. "What help do you seek?"

Caly motioned for Mandy to take out the bottle. She did and unfolded her hand so the woman could see.

"Do you mind?" Zoe asked, placing her hand over the small bottle. She turned it over in her hand and lifted it to her nose. "It's a common bronze potion bottle. How did you come across it?"

"It was given to me," answered Mandy.

"Hmm… It was a resourceful witch. What's inside here isn't a potion. It's magic."

Mandy was confused, *Isn't a potion magic?* "Can you clarify?" asked Mandy.

She placed the bottle back in Mandy's palm. "Think of it like fairy dust. Trapped in here is someone's condensed magic. This was traditionally done when a witch's powers were siphoned, but siphoning hasn't been common practice for over a hundred years."

Mandy was more confused. *Whose magic is trapped in the bottle?*

"Come with me, let's talk in back. Discussion of trapped siphoned magic can be dangerous, especially when we don't know whom it belongs," she said, gliding past the counter and into a back room with a table, a few chairs, a desk, and a back door.

"Now, how exactly did you get this?"

Joel slid his fingers between Mandy's and took her hand. She wasn't offering the entire story. For sixteen years she'd been hidden, taken from her family and her magic-bound parents. Heck, it might be their magic inside the bottle. "A few weeks ago, my mother was murdered and night witches surrounded and destroyed my home. These wolves rescued me. I've been with them since. Last night, the bottle appeared in my hand after the wolves defended me from an attacking silver-haired witch."

Zoe's eyes widened at the mention of the silver-haired witch, but she didn't proceed to talk about her. "I was hoping it would give me an idea, but it doesn't. You carry magic of your own. I sensed your energy the moment you walked into the store. The magic is strong, but I can't read it, and you're clearly not a witch, but it's most likely the reason a witch is hunting you," she said with a grim face.

Mandy twisted her lips. The witch knew something about Silver Hair but wasn't forthcoming with her knowledge. She decided to give her a bit more. She already sensed something and maybe wasn't being completely honest with her either. "I don't have magic, but carry magic in the form of an amulet."

"The amethyst Slayer. Yes, the stone carries spelled magic, but you have your own magic." she said, playing with a ring on her finger.

Her parents were witches, so it made sense, even though Mandy wasn't one. Some genetic combination gave her magic too. Noting Zoe's nervous fidgeting with her ring, she wondered how much she knew, but couldn't think of anything to say except, "I have magic?"

She took a deep breath. "All Slayers have magic. They are born into the light witch blood line that spelled their amulet. Seven amulets, seven light witch bloodlines, but your magic is a little different," she paused and the room became very quiet. Then Zoe offered, "I can test it without opening the bottle."

She mixed an herb concoction and placed the bottle onto her desk and surrounded it with candles, then sprinkled the herbal mixture over it and chanted in a language Mandy didn't recognize.

Almost immediately, a violet-white glow surrounded the bottle, followed by the scent of gardenia. A black cloud formed beneath the violet-white light and moved upward, mingling with the light. They danced together around the bottle.

Zoe's eyes widened, as did everyone else's as they watched the display of darkness twisting with the light. Then it disintegrated. She took a step backwards. "I've never seen anything like that. Light magic doesn't mix with dark. Take it, get it out of here. Get it out my store!" she said, her voice shaking.

The doorbell rang as a customer entered the store. Mandy grabbed the bottle and shoved it into the opposite front pocket to the amulet while she asked, "So the magic is good and bad?"

Zoe took more steps backward away from Mandy, and Joel tugged at her hand as he stepped towards the back door.

"We have something else… " said Miranda. Her voice trailing off as Zoe's eyes shot bullets towards her.

Caly shot Miranda the same glare she'd given her the day they went on their three-wheel adventure and took her to the fruit trees. "I'm sorry. We didn't know," Caly and Miranda said in unison as they walked towards the door.

Mandy responded to Joel and fell in step with him as they exited the shop. "I'm sorry," Mandy offered, her eyes pleading with the sisters. "I didn't know."

Miranda took her vacant hand. "How could you? None of us knew, and neither did she or she wouldn't have tested it. Our family has a history with hers and everything will be fine."

"But I'm carrying dark magic in my pocket. I don't even want the thing. And what about the book?" Mandy replied in a quivering voice as she fought the fear rising inside her like a volcano about to erupt.

Joel let go of her hand and wrapped an arm around her shoulder. "We'll sort it out over food. No one's eaten all day."

She adored him; always a calm voice of reason. The group walked around the strip mall and into the pizza place. The aroma of garlic and bread made Mandy's stomach grumble in hunger.

They ordered a pizza and were talking among themselves, brainstorming what they should do next, when a man with red hair and a goatee took a seat in the booth next to them. Immediately they changed the subject.

A dark-haired waitress brought their pizza and slid it onto the table and a young man dropped off a stack of plates. "Be right back to refill those drinks," said the waitress with a smile and wink.

After the waitress came and went, the man in the booth beside them turned his head and placed his arm on the top of the cushion.

"I think I can help you," he whispered.

Disturbed by his apparent eavesdropping, Mandy narrowed her eyes at him. "We don't need any help," she smarted.

He licked his lips and pulled on his goatee. "I don't mean to interrupt your meal, but I overheard you in Magik Essence. I'm a witch and it seems you need one." He kept his voice low.

Their eyes shifted from one to the other. Mandy didn't feel any negative energy rising from him, and from the looks on the wolves' faces neither did they.

Joel spoke, "Take a seat, join us."

The man slipped out of his booth and next to Caly, who sat across from Mandy. "I'm Henrick." He cleared his throat. "It isn't every day you see a group of wolves escorting a Slayer."

Mandy scrunched her face. She didn't know if that was a threat or an observation. Either way, he knew what they were. "It's not an everyday situation that brings us together. Now, you said you can help. How?"

"I'm a light witch, but not a strong one. I didn't find my magic until I was nearly eighteen and never learned to control the light. I left a few holes in unfortunate places, so I dabble in potions and spells mainly. I can't help you with the magic in your bottle." He paused. "Dark and light shouldn't mix. I may be able to help you with your other problem."

"Last night we were attacked by a night witch. I managed to get a hold of her for an instant before she vanished-- long enough to get a mouthful of her cloth dress and scratch her leg," Joel said, keeping his voice low.

The man yanked at his goatee again. "A wolf biting a night witch. Interesting. And you kept the cloth and blood?"

Mandy nodded. "Can you analyze it or something?"

He let go of his goatee. "I can."

Chapter 20

Alison and the Slayers

Alison sifted through the clothes in her closet searching for something to wear. She settled on a new pair of jeans her mom picked up for her with a pattern embroidered on the back pockets and a loose blouse with fringes hanging from the bottom. Cool air swept past her causing her to shiver. "Alistair, is that you?" she whispered.

She focused her energy and entered the spirit realm. Standing in front of her was Alistair. This meant the witch was back. Her heart pounded and thumped against her ribcage. She dreaded going back into the tunnels.

"She is back, angry an' injured," he said, his round eyes bulging at his words.

Only one part of his statement stood out to her – injured. "She's injured?"

"Thee 'eard my words."

She nodded. "I'll get the others. Keep an eye on her." She scrunched her face and painted on a faux smile.

"Blimey, hurry it up," he said in a curt voice.

"We will," she said as his form disintegrated.

She brought herself out of the spirit world and stepped out of the closet, laid her clothes on her bed, and jumped two feet in the air when she heard a man behind her say, "The witch is fuming. We need to get in there now."

She turned around and jumped again when she spotted Tim the Shiftling standing buck naked near her open closet door. Grabbing the top blanket on her bed she threw it at him. "What the heck? Cover up!"

He caught the blanket and wrapped it around his waist like a towel. She'd have to wash that before using it again.

"We don't shift with clothes on you know. They don't exactly make them in lady bug size," he said, sarcasm in every word as they dripped from his mouth.

She crossed her arms across her chest in dismay and frustration that supes always came to her. *Why not the other Slayers?* "She's back. Do you have a plan?"

"Not only is she back, but she's madder than a bee at a bear stealing honey."

"What do we do?"

"Gather your crew and meet at my house. I suspect you know the one." In the flash of an eye he vanished, replaced by a lady bug.

She scooped him up and let him out the door. Her mom was in the kitchen, humming as she poured waffle mix into the maker and pressed the top down.

"What are you doing today, Ally?" she asked between hums.

She couldn't tell her the truth exactly. "Hanging out with friends. Lacey and Rodham." *Oh and*

Alistair, Tim, and a bunch of Shifters, Adrian, and a nasty witch. "The waffles smell good," she added as she grabbed a crunchy slice of bacon off a plate.

"That sounds nice," said her mom, an edge to her voice as she swatted Alison's hand

There was a tension in her mother's voice and a painted smile on her face. *Does she know? She couldn't. Not possible,* Alison convinced herself.

Al, I'm coming over, Rodham said in a rushed voice in her head.

That settled it. *She* was a hub for the paranormal and supernatural not St. Augustine. Within seconds he knocked on the door.

"Who is it?" asked her mother as Alison opened the door.

"Rodham. I'll be back in a few minutes for breakfast." Thinking quick, she followed up with, "We decided to start taking morning walks on the weekend." And she shut the door before her mother could ask her any more questions. Electricity crackled between their energies. *I heard. The witch returned.*

Yes she has.

He shook his head and they briskly walked toward the man-made lake's edge, centered in the middle of their apartment complex. His face grew serious. *Last night my mind was trapped inside a three-way call. No, it wasn't three-way, but more like two people having a conversation and my line crossed theirs. It was staticky and I haven't really made out the message, but I think I was there on purpose like someone hijacked my mind so I could listen.*

Alison turned her head from the lake to Rodham. His green eyes large. *A witch? Maybe a dark witch?*

I don't think so. It was a familiar sensation. I think Veronica pulled me in. I don't know how. If her magic is strong enough to pull me in, then wouldn't it make sense she'd be strong enough to break free?

Alison bit her upper lip and thought about that for a second. Since they killed the colony of Bloodseekers, Rodham hadn't had his amulet until now. Did she know or sense it in some way? They'd all considered Veronica kidnapped and immobilized, but maybe she wasn't, or was waiting for something. But what? *Why not break free if she could?*

Veronica's a strong witch and we've considered her the victim, but what if she's not? Maybe she played us?

I don't think so. I don't think she's trapped like we thought, but I don't think she played us. The other voice belonged to another Slayer. We have a certain signature to our brain waves. I couldn't figure out which one, but it wasn't me, you, Lacey, or Adrian.

Topaz! Alison's brain shouted. They had the amulet, now they needed the Slayer.

He shrugged.

I had a visit this morning from Alistair and Tim. We need to get everyone together and meet at Tim's.

I got that covered, he mind talked and gave her a wink.

Within the hour, they were all gathered at Tim's. All the Slayers, Cody, and a few Shiftlings devising a course of action. Lacey and Cody could hold back the water. Adrian had his ability to teleport and would move in and grab Veronica when she was found. The Shiftlings could transform into tiny flying creatures such as bats and moths, so they had an aerial view and could fly into small places and through cracks that Alison and Rodham couldn't. Rodham could tap into the witch's brain signature and find her. He wasn't sure if he'd hear her thoughts, as night witches had the ability to cloak them. Alison could make her and Rodham invisible so they could wander through the tunnels completely invisible.

Everyone dispersed and the Slayers geared up, arming themselves with their swords and stakes for another battle against the Bloodseekers – this time the ones guarding Veronica.

Chapter 21

Mandy

They had to be more candid with Henrick so he could analyze the blood. The sample was only enough for one spell, so he needed to know the witch's target. The group gathered around the table in his garage as he mixed a sample of Mandy's blood with the sample from the witch and chanted words in a language she recognized as the same as Zoe from Magik Essence had used.

The blood swirled together then shot in a straight line toward Mandy, stopping at the edge of the table. Her eyes widened, as did Henrick's.

He scratched his head then pulled his goatee. "You're not going to like this, but it seems you and the witch are related. I don't understand how that's possible." He paused for a second. "As a Slayer, you're from a light witch bloodline."

Mandy was surprised, yet not that surprised. She knew her biological father was a night witch and her twin was a witch. What boggled her mind was that Carlito said her twin showed signs of being a light witch and destroyed Bloodseekers both on her own and with the group of Slayers. *If the Silver Haired witch who sneaked into her head and attacked her from the inside out was her sister, then who was the other witch who gave her the bottle of trapped magic?*

"Like how related?" asked Caly.

She stole the words right out of Mandy's mouth.

"That I can't tell you, but a relative close enough your blood mingles, becoming one. Most blood, even with two witches of the same light, will attract but will not mingle even in the same bloodline if it's one step removed such as a cousin, aunt, or uncle. Witch blood of opposite light will repel. When the blood is of the same light and closely related, such as immediate family, it mingles and will move in the direction of the family member – you," he stated, pointing at Mandy.

Her brain was muddled and confused.

Are you there? asked a male voice inside Mandy's head. She ignored it, thinking her brain was playing tricks on her.

"So you're saying a parent or sibling?" Mandy asked, not needing his confirmation. She knew.

"Or grandparent."

You can't push me out. I'm a Slayer and our brains are linked. We need you. Go to the Cathedral Basilica in St. Augustine. Your sword is there. You'll see its light, follow it. I'll tell you later where to meet us. We need you tonight, said the same male voice who intruded in her mind only moments earlier. *What the heck? Should I respond?* All this mind junk was upsetting her. How dare anyone reach inside her mind? And how did she know beyond a doubt he was a Slayer? Maybe it was a trick from the witch who appeared to be her sister.

Who are you? How are you inside my head? And how do I know you're a Slayer and not a witch trying to trick me?

Slow down. I'm Rodham and telepathy is my game. I wear the emerald amulet. My mind discussion shouldn't send negative energy but feel natural. A witch's would feel forced.

She felt intruded on, but the voice did feel natural. *Ok, maybe.*

You block your mind well. I've been trying to contact you since last night when I was forced into a conversation between you and a witch.

You were there?

Kind of. I was more a listener and wasn't given the opportunity to communicate, but I'm sure a friend of ours was responsible for it. She's a witch and has been trapped by a night witch for a few weeks now. I don't know how she knew who you were, or why she brought us into a three-way, but she gave you something. I haven't told any Slayer about the details of the conversation.

You heard it?

Very clear. Whatever she gave you, it's important. Keep it close and safe.

"Where to?" asked Joel, bringing Mandy out of the telepathic conversation.

On auto-pilot, Mandy followed the others back to the Escalade and climbed into the front seat. The charcoal-colored dash with wooden and silver trim in front of her. "What?"

"Where are we going?" reiterated Joel in a calm voice.

"The Cathedral Basilica in St. Augustine," she stated as she pulled the seat belt around her and clicked it in place.

Joel engaged the engine and she set the GPS. Her life had been nonstop since leaving Wolf Manor and she missed it. She'd spent her time there frustrated, but now she'd take it back in a heartbeat. *What did my parents get me into?*

Within a couple hours, Mandy was sneaking into the church. Not really sneaking, she went through the front door, but struck off into an area marked for staff. She followed the light as Rodham said and found her sword easily. The problem was getting to it. It wasn't out in open waiting for her, but hidden somewhere inside a locked storage closet.

She reached her mind out, searching for Rodham, and sent a message she hoped he heard. *I'm in the Cathedral, but my sword is behind locked doors. I can't get inside.*

He promptly replied and she felt relieved. *No problem. Send me a mental picture.*

She wasn't sure how to do that, so turned in a circle around the area. A white, comforting light swallowed her up. The next thing, she was on the opposite side of the door, staring into a dark closet surrounded by swirls of violet, orange, and blue light. Along with the glow of her amulet, she had enough light to see. The closet was large and filled with artifacts. Old stuff she assumed belonged to the church. The swords' glows emanated from behind a shelf. One thing at a time, she moved the items, wishing she had a wolf with her. They were much stronger.

Can you see it? We can get it out.

Why didn't I think of that? If they transported me inside the closet, surely they could transport the sword.

Because it's all new to you.

You heard that.

Of course. We're linked. Send another mental image.

She sighed and stared in the direction of the sword. *It's somewhere behind that.*

We got them.

The white light shot towards the pile and out rose three long, shining silver swords. One had an amethyst stone in the center that matched the one on the amulet safely tucked in her pocket. The light carried them towards her. She gripped the heavy handle of the amethyst sword and energy traveled through her, igniting her body in a swirl of violet light. White light enveloped her and she and the sword were dropped outside the Cathedral.

How did you do that?

I didn't do anything. You bonded with it. My gift is mind communication. You can thank Adrian the teleporter later. We're a team.

Chapter 22

Alison and the Slayers

The sun sank below the horizon and darkness settled as the Slayers and Cody made their way back to the tunnel. Waiting for them was a group of Shiftlings.

A thin woman with auburn hair greeted them. Her face drooped. "She's moved."

"What?" asked Adrian. "When?"

"Only moments ago. We don't yet know where they went, but we should know something soon. Our scout was able to slip past the Seekers and into Veronica's pocket when the night witch dropped the shield and teleported them out," she said.

"So we wait," said Lacey.

The auburn-headed Shiftling nodded.

Alison took the opportunity to completely invisibilize herself and enter the spirit world, calling for Alistair. When she didn't immediately hear from him, she sucked in a deep breath and sank down beneath the tunnel's entrance using her light to look into the rank musty tunnel. She shivered as the water's cold tongue licked her shoes and sank in through the seams.

"Thee called," asked Alistair's familiar voice.

In front of her stood the short, round-faced Boggart. "Alistair. Did you hear the witch say anything before she left?"

"Mumblin' under 'er breff," he responded, leaping from the water to the pavement at street level.

She bit her lip. "What did she mumble?"

"Ai, when the shield came down, she mumbled 'Sturdy walls of the south take us to the mouth.'"

"Thank you! Did she pull everything out?"

He nodded and gripped her hand as she lifted herself onto the dry platform. "Da' stinky beasts are gone an' everything else."

She thanked him and sent Rodham a message. *What can this mean: 'sturdy walls of the south take us to the mouth'?*

I don't know. The fort maybe?

She'd visited the fort with her Gran and mother. Shaped like a huge box, with wide-open space and several rooms long with narrow staircases and walkways, made it a great place to hide Veronica and defend herself. *Let's find out.*

She joined the other Slayers. The warm white light enveloped them and dumped them behind Castillo de San Marcos Fort, along Matanzas Bay. The sounds of St. Augustine filled their ears. Music, people, and cars all on the other side of the street that divided the Fort from the historic city.

The overwhelming pheromone stench the Bloodseekers carry was absent, which meant the witch probably wasn't there. They split up anyway and searched the grounds, then met in the back where they landed and snuck into the fort.

Inside, it was calm and quiet. Alison readied her sword, as it was far too quiet, and crept along the top edge by the cannons, her ears on full alert. Rodham went in the other direction, and Lacey and Adrian strode to the open middle, hunting along the inside edges.

An hour later, they'd searched every inch of the fort. None of them turned up anything. It was lifeless and still giving Alison an eerie feeling. The witch wasn't there. She'd have done something by now or Bloodseekers would be awaiting an attack; but there was nothing and Rodham hadn't felt any brain waves but theirs. The witch could cloak hers, but not the Seekers'.

"This place is empty," spilled Adrian, dropping his sword to his side.

"We don't want to underestimate her. We know she's strong," urged Lacey. Her eyes wide, the yellow pupils sparked with electricity.

Alison interrupted. "A trap. We need to get out of here, now!" she urged.

Rodham's eyes lit up. "Not a trap. She isn't here. I almost forgot about it, but there's another fort, much smaller, to the south. It sits at the mouth where the river opens to the Atlantic Ocean. 'Sturdy walls of the south take us to the mouth'!"

Their eyes widened and Alison pulled out her phone and looked up the location of the fort. "It's surrounded by nothing. It's perfect!" She widened the map. "We can sneak in on the north end without being noticed. We have to walk a distance."

Adrian nodded. "We'll make it work. Have your swords at the ready. We don't know what we're walking into or how far out she has Bloodseekers."

Their eyes connected in a blinding array of electricity and light. Adrian nodded, a dark flap of straight hair covering one of his eyes and sliding toward the other.

The white light enveloped the group and landed them on the north end of Fort Matanzas on the edge of a swampy lake.

Alison pulled her already wet sneakers out of the muck, wishing she had a pair of boots for the terrain but was glad that at least she wasn't wearing flip-flops or sandals. The area was nothing but trees and swamp land. She caught a large whiff of the Bloodseekers' morbid stench as a gentle breeze washed over her.

The sun was quickly setting, darkening the sky. Using the trees for cover and the pounding of the surf as a guide, they trudged toward the coast. The stench of Bloodseekers stronger with each step. Dark clouds formed south over the ocean, and the air grew muggier.

Stop! I feel strong Bloodseeker brain waves. They know we're here.

They halted their steps and formed a circle with swords drawn. The stench of Bloodseekers filled Alison's nostrils and she cringed.

They've surrounded us. The group is young and doesn't have battle experience. When they attack, Adrian will teleport

*us out of the middle and disperse us outside their group. This
will confuse them. Be ready to fight.*

Leaves crunched around them and, through the
trees, a band of Bloodseekers surrounded them.
Alison's hands were sweaty against her sword. The
Seekers moved in closer, making a circle around
them. Alison counted fourteen.

Bloodseekers hid among humans using beauty.
Perfectly toned, flawless bodies; shiny, radiant hair
and eyes. But Slayers saw them for what they were --
nasty, deformed beasts.

Their sharp fangs protruded from their gums,
and long, twisted nails extended from their
fingertips. Deep black pits filled their eye sockets. In
exchange for immortality, they became hideous
nocturnal creatures.

"There is nothing here for you. You're not even
a tasty morsel. Why do you come?" asked a Seeker.
Her speech slow and pronounced.

Are they trying to work a deal? thought Alison.

*No, they're trying to buy time. More are coming. We need
to move them in closer,* Rodham sent to the group.

Lacey baited them. "We're here for you. Your
stench carries over the land and we smelled you
from the city."

A few Seekers moved closer, drool dripping
from their jaws.

"I'll rip that amulet off your neck and suck you
dry!" growled a Seeker.

"Try it," she said as he rushed towards her,
stopping only a couple feet away. She didn't flinch.
She raised her hand and lifted him off the ground,

depositing him onto a jagged stump. He screamed in agony as it pierced his heart.

That did it. Losing one of their own ticked them off, and they rushed towards them. Bloodseekers were notoriously stupid, but quick. Lacey held them back as Adrian teleported them out of the ring of Bloodseekers.

With no time to think only react, Alison swung her sword at a male Seeker as he turned around, appearing disoriented. She missed his neck but slashed through his middle and he toppled to the ground. Without missing a beat, she brought her sword down across his neck and separated it from his body.

One by one, they took them down, until a pile of quickly decaying Seekers covered the ground. Alison took a deep breath.

More are coming and this group is much older!

Chapter 23

The bolt of lightning shot through the sky, followed within minutes by a blast of thunder, and the dark foreboding clouds moved quickly onto land. Able to tap into their magic and channel it through their amulets the Slayers were a formidable group.

The area was crawling with Bloodseekers. They were like roaches; no matter how many they killed, there were always more. Alison used her power to cloak them from the Seekers. Outnumbered, they chose not to fight until help came in the form of Shiftlings and the new Slayer. They moved through the woods with light footsteps. The Seekers having excellent hearing, they had to take gentle steps.

At the edge of the woods, Matanzas Fort in full view, they stopped, regrouped, and waited. Rodham made contact with Cody who had stayed at the tunnels with the Shiftlings. He alerted them they were on the way.

Another crack of lighting streamed from the sky as the Shiftlings in the form of large animals -- a cougar, a panther, a lion, and a bear -- landed with only a tiny rustle of the grass but it was enough to alert the Bloodseekers. Their fine-tuned hearing picked up on it and a rush of them plowed forward.

Adrian set the Slayers on a teleportation cycle around the Seekers to confuse them the way his great uncle did before passing the amulet on. It was Rodham's idea as he'd fought alongside him. The extra advantage was their invisibility.

Alison ran forward and ripped her blade across a Seeker's face, his skin falling away from the gash. The panther jumped him from behind and she plunged her sword into his heart. He twitched, then stopped moving completely. She whipped around and caught another across the neck.

Lacey lifted one off the ground and set him down as Rodham's sword slashed into the air, catching Lacey's victim along with Rodham's. Another Seeker flew over the tree tops, landing with a thud in a tree. Branches cracked and broke under his weight, jabbing his flesh and entering his heart as he dropped to the ground.

Their screams reverberated in Alison's head as one fell after another. These evil beasts were relentless. The Slayer teleportation cycle shifted and they vanished into the white light, turning up somewhere else.

Electricity and balls of light exploded from Cody's finger tips, melting his Bloodseeker victims from the inside out.

The massive bear picked one up and, shoving his claw into her chest, ripped out her heart, tossing it -- and her -- several feet with no more effort than tossing a soda can. Alison twirled and dodged as one went down and another took its place.

A blast of electricity sizzled behind Alison and threw the Seeker high in the air and he landed with a thunk more than twenty feet in front of her. She turned her head while whipping her blade across a Seeker and, when he fell, her mother stood on the other side. Time froze and she blinked her eyes, hoping they were playing tricks on her. A Bloodseeker rushed her mother from behind. Alison screamed, "Mom!" and rushed towards her mother who shrank to the ground. She didn't have the time to process that her mom was a light witch, only enough time to react. Alison reached out her arm, then the white light enveloped her as the teleportation cycle moved again.

When the white light dissipated, she found her mother and ran towards her, lopping off the heads of every Seeker standing in her way. Before she reached her, three distinct howls broadcast through the air and caught her attention. She stopped, turning her head towards the howls. Running towards them were three wolves, followed by a pack of large dogs of all breeds. They formed a V, and riding on the largest wolf who led the group was a teen who, even from where she stood, looked like Veronica. A violet glow encompassed her.

The black clouds swirled overhead. Torrents of rain suddenly fell as if someone dumped a never ending bucket of water on them from the sky. In the distance, she noted several night witches lined up on the shoreline, their arms stretched toward the heavens.

Alison squinted her eyes and, through the rain, saw that in the hand of the girl riding the wolf was a chain and the source of violet light. She dropped it over her neck, and when it hit her chest a blast of violet light curled around her as a lightning bolt struck the girl. She pirouetted off the wolf's back and into the sky, violet light and eddying flames surrounding her. The fall out of her light traveled over the Bloodseekers and night witches, engulfing them in fire. A fire the rain didn't have any effect on. Their cries echoed in her ears even after they turned to dust.

Alison glanced downward at her mom and collapsed to the ground beside her. She laid her head against her chest and felt her heartbeat, steady but slow. Tears dropped from her eyes and someone fell onto her knees beside her. The teen that rose off the wolf in a violet light storm.

She pressed her palms against the wound in Alison's mother's shoulder. A glow of violet electricity traveled into the wound and it sealed and became whole in front of Alison's eyes. She gasped in awe and stared into the violet eyes of the amethyst Slayer – the healer -- electricity buzzing between them. Alison clutched her mother's hand and stared at the damage surrounding them. Fallen Bloodseekers covered the earth and tree branches sizzled and dropped. The lush ground was singed brown. The lightning intensified the bonding with her amulet and destroyed everything as far as her eye could see, including the gang of night witches spread along the shoreline.

The sky cleared and the stars shone brightly. The rain quit. Alison hadn't moved. She watched the amethyst Slayer move from one injured comrade to the next. Light passing over their bodies, healing any wounds.

Time, that for a moment stood still, now sped and Alison helped her mother stand then wrapped her arms around her. "Mom, what are you doing here? This is dangerous."

Her mother's lips smiled softly and she placed her hands on Alison's cheeks. "That's why I'm here," she said.

"You're OK," came a voice Alison recognized in spades but didn't associate with supes.

She peered downward towards the voice. A large Rottweiler stood beside her mother. "Mr. Tucker?"

"Alison," his mouth moved and the words flowed from it, but it didn't seem natural for an animal to talk. She shrugged and the group walked towards the other.

The battle wasn't over and Veronica wasn't free. They still needed to defeat the silver-haired witch.

Chapter 24

Mandy

The group listened to Mandy's story in awe that she and Veronica were sisters, even though they were identical in every way except Mandy's violet eyes.

Mandy led the way with Joel by her side as she and the other Slayers stormed the fort. She was finding her sister and felt her presence stronger than ever before, meaning she was very close. The Shiftlings and wolves guarded the tiny fort from the outside with the light witches and worked together to trace the night witch's magic and halt it.

The fort was so small there were only five cannons and a few rooms. Mandy and Joel stood in the center and called her out as she turned in a circle. "There's nowhere for you to go. I don't even care about destroying you. All I want is my sister."

"She's not yours," said the witch. "If you remove the wolf I'll think about it." Her voice came from every direction.

Mandy turned to Joel. "It's OK."

Reluctantly, he moved away from the middle and joined the Slayers.

"Go outside, wolf!" The silver-haired witch shouted and it echoed off the stone walls.

He snarled and thrashed his tail as he went outside the fort.

They'd traced two sources of magic, but couldn't decipher which one was Veronica's. Their signatures were too similar.

Mandy remembered what Hendrick said, and it all made sense, every bit of it. 'You're not going to like this, but it seems you and the witch are related. I don't understand how that's possible." and "As a Slayer, you're from a light witch bloodline,' were Hendrick's words after the silver-haired witch's blood shot straight at her. Sibling rivalry – it was that simple. "I know who you are, sister. We were ripped from each other and never given the chance to be a family, but we can start fresh."

She witnessed each Slayers' jaw drop and eyes widen.

"You're tricking me and it won't work," said the silver-haired witch. Mandy listened carefully, trying to determine her location but couldn't. However, she got an idea.

Can Adrian teleport them both into the open? she asked Rodham.

A few seconds later he responded. *The witches have their location and he's going to work with them to pull them out. Together, they should be strong enough.*

A white funnel of light flickered only a few feet from Mandy. *You're going to feel a tug on your energy as I funnel it through me to help transport us.* The female head voice took Mandy by surprise but this time she knew it was her twin, Veronica, who also gave her the tiny bottle of siphoned magic.

A stream of violet connected with the flickering funnel of white, pulling Mandy with it. Lacey lifted her hands and tugged on Mandy to keep her from entering it. Mandy felt as if she was the rope in a game of tug-of-war or Stretch Armstrong. After what seemed like forever, but was merely seconds, the light dissipated and a few feet from her stood her sister trapped inside a clear bubble along with the silver-haired witch.

She fell to the ground onto her hands and knees, drained of energy, staring into the blue eyes of her identical twin.

"I knew you were lying," snarled Mandy's silver-haired witch sister.

She glanced at her, her violet eyes the same color as Mandy's now, and smiled at her warmly. "I'm proud to meet you both." Her arms went out from under her and she collapsed completely, her body aching in pain as a violet swirl of light exited the bubble and moved towards her and dissipated. Next to her stood her twin. She placed her hands on her back and the warm energy of the violet light went back into her.

"What, you think you can trap me?" called the silver-haired witch.

Mandy glanced in her direction, but said nothing.

"It took you long enough sister. Sorry I had to siphon you. It was the only way to get out and save our little sister too. Two souls as one," Veronica said with a smirk.

Then Veronica turned and swapped glances with the Slayers. "Hey guys. It's been a month and I had to do most of the work!"

Mandy blinked. The crumpling pain and light leaving her body was familiar. It happened when she found the door at Wolf Manor. She'd done it before. She touched her sister on the shoulder. Electricity buzzed through her arm. "That's not the first time you siphoned me!"

"No, it's not. I needed your energy," she smirked.

Mandy stood wordless. She saved her sister who'd been using her energy to do what?

Veronica strolled towards the Slayers who were happy to have their frenemy back and admitted they missed her sparkling personality. Veronica could have left on her own, as the silver-haired sister, Arama, had distributed her energy into too many activities, therefore weakening it, but chose not to as it might have destroyed her, Arama, and their parents.

When she'd first arrived she had them trapped then moved them, but not before Veronica siphoned their parents' bound powers and trapped them in the bottle. There were no answers yet as to how their parents' had another child without other witches knowing about it… or did they use her? Mandy hoped those answers would come soon.

Veronica kept the bottle hidden until she finally got through to Mandy and passed it to her. Her plan was to restore their powers, but she needed all of them on the same page to do that. She didn't know how long it would take to turn Arama and find their parents. No matter how long, she wasn't giving up and neither was Mandy, the Slayers, Shiftlings, or the wolves. Together they'd fight.

Now Mandy understood. She'd siphoned her energy to save their family. "So what do we do with her?" asked Mandy.

"I'm taking her home after we bind her powers and set up a few heavy duty wards around the house. You can join us."

Mandy glanced at Joel, then Tim. "Wolves and Shiftlings under the same roof? We want to keep the peace. There's plenty of places we can rent."

Joel, in his beautiful human form, walked towards Mandy and snaked one arm around Mandy's neck and another around her waist, pulling her close. He pressed his mouth against hers. Energy coursed through her body and she welcomed his tongue inside her mouth.

"What…ever," Veronica mocked as she turned on her heel towards the huddle of other witches.

Chapter 25

Alison

Alison and her mom returned home, both safe and healthy, and had a heart to heart. Her mother'd known she was a witch from the time she was thirteen, when her powers first showed themselves. She accidentally electrocuted a student who was terrorizing a friend. She didn't mean to do it and didn't understand her magic. Upset, she punched the girl in the face and she went down. Electricity buzzing through her body as she convulsed.

Alison chuckled inwardly at the thought of her mother in a school fight. The girl survived, but with the enormity of the magic and her lack of control, she stuffed it away and swore to never use it again. And she didn't until she learned about Alison and the Slayers. It was Mr. Tucker, a Shiftling. He knew Alison was a Slayer and when he bumped into her mother at the post office he felt her magic.

Even though Slayers come from light witch bloodlines, most their ancestors don't develop their magic. He informed her of the Slayers and Bloodseekers and Alison's involvement. That led Alison's mother to question Gran's rapid aging. It put everything in perspective for her and made sense, even though it sounded like a vampire sitcom or one of the books Alison read.

Angrier than a bear in a trap, she went to Gran who confirmed everything. That's when she told Gran about her powers and decided she had to learn to control them. Mr. Tucker helped her out as he had a few light witch friends, and she spent time daily wielding her light and learning to use it.

Alison and her mother Skyped Gran to inform her of the day's events. When she answered, her eyes lit for a second as she saw her daughter and grandaughter as a united front. A warm smile crossed her face.

Taking turns, they relayed the story without missing a beat, including the twins and the story of their parents. As Alison talked, she remembered her Gran once telling her a story, thought of more as a fable, about a light and a night witch that fell in love, only in the story her Gran told they were killed. In reality, their powers were bound and now siphoned by their eldest daughter -- Veronica. And they believed they would be turned over to the sorceress if they weren't already.

Alison didn't know if she'd ever trust Arama, and everything weird about Veronica and her powers now made sense. She was a witch of both light and darkness and so was Arama. Their own father was a night witch who couldn't be too terribly evil if he fell in love with a light witch and risked his life to save his daughters. There was good Binside them and she had to believe that Veronica and Mandy would find a way to release it inside their sister.

"I'm proud of you and the other Slayers. Together, you have gone further than any group before you. The five of you have managed to unite all supernatural creatures on earth into a formidable army against a common enemy. Light and dark have combined in the souls of these three sisters for a special reason. You are the group who will together find and defeat the sorceress, but remember light and dark can live at peace with one another just as the moon and stars shine at night."

Gran's speech slowed and her lips halted. Her dull amber eyes froze. Alison's heart dropped to the floor and she turned to her mother. Their eyes filled with horror.

"Mom, Mom! Gran! There's something wrong," Alison said as tears poured down her cheeks.

Her mother swallowed and sniffled as she called the police station nearest Gran's home. They made a home call, finding her dead. Alison and her mother wept together. And Alison knew she'd hung on, waiting for that call. With the confidence that the new Slayers wouldn't simply destroy the sorceress, but unite all supernaturals on Earth and peace would follow.

They didn't waste time, but flew to Virginia and had Gran's body cremated. Bringing her ashes home, they took half of them and spread them over Alda's by the St. Augustine Lighthouse so both their lights could shine together forever.

Epilogue

The Monday before Thanksgiving...

Alison sat in the front seat of the car as her mother drove them to the airport in Orlando to pick up Vicky. She watched the trees pass in a mess of green. Arama's personality was every bit as charming as Veronica's and she seemed to be coming around. She'd expected Mandy to be the topaz Slayer and was more shocked then anything that she had violet light. She glanced at her mom and was happy Mandy was the amethyst Slayer and had the ability to heal her wound. She didn't even have a scar. Her mom parked the car and together they walked into the airport.

Vicky's flight was on time and they met her outside baggage claim. Alison's bright garnet eyes lit up the room and she and Vicky rushed towards each other, wrapping their arms around each other.

"You shine like a red light bulb. Can't you turn it down a bit?" said Vicky, a cheek to cheek smile on her face.

"You see it?" The smile gone from Alison's face.

"Yeah," Vicky paused as her brain engaged. "OMG! I never saw it on the phone. I shouldn't see it now. Unless I'm... a ... OMG!"

Their eyes widened as their gazes met.

Once home, Alison took out the topaz amulet. Mandy had the journal. They figured it was safer to keep them apart. Immediately, Vicky felt its warmth and call to her.

Rodham's voice beamed into Alison's head. *Arama fessed up. We know where their parents are. The sorceress has them...*

The GHOST Within

Elle Klass

Prologue

The late afternoon sun spread across the most vibrant natural garden Miguel had ever laid eyes on. But its appearance was superseded by the pain he felt marching through it. Many had suffered great agony. He couldn't see it, but its combined sorrow clutched his heart and yanked. The sword on his back was easily accessible but wouldn't be needed until the sun set beneath the horizon and blackness swathed the land. Hopefully, he'd find what he was looking for sooner.

It was instinct that brought him there. An impulse that intensified with the proximity of his sword. He was chosen, and took on the responsibility with pride as any soldier would. Swallowing his fear and the pain of many that rested on his heart, he carefully moved through the colorful jungle-like field of wildflowers and other flora.

He halted when the leaves rustled in a beeline towards him. His hand on the butt of the sword, he grasped its handle ready to lop off the head of whatever was headed his way. His legs and body angled in a fighting stance, the leaves moved past and around him, but no creature. It was only a late afternoon breeze. Letting out a deep breath, he continued.

The trickle of water captured his attention. He stopped and closed his eyes, using his sense of hearing to determine its direction. Opening his eyes, he moved towards it, the afternoon sun lowering on the horizon.

A bright, golden glow rose above the wildflowers. Everything inside him urged him to run towards it and he hurried his pace. The ache of hundreds of souls' agony flooded his humanity and clutched his head and chest, immobilizing him. He was close. Squeezing his eyes tight, he attempted to push the pain away and forced his legs to move forward. The sun was quickly sinking and he didn't have much time.

One foot in front of the other, he fought the misery embedding itself inside him and strained onward, the natural spring in sight. He only needed to take a few more steps. The seconds passed slowly and the gripping pain lowered him to his knees. *It's right there Miguel,* he chanted as he drove onward. The sun drifted beneath the horizon. The only light above pulsing from the stars overhead, even the moon was hiding tonight.

Flat on his belly, he stretched his arm to the water. In the distance he heard them. The pounding of many footfalls vibrated against his chest. The water was warm and gave him the strength to pull himself forward, dropping into the spring. The energy consumed him and the golden glow soaked into him as he submerged himself in the water.

The flora around him parted, and at least twenty people rushed toward the spring. He pushed into the center and dove beneath the surface. He had to find it, and quick. He held his breath and searched with his eyes as he scanned the dirt. The glow radiated to his right. Coming up for air, he took a large gulp and his eyes expanded as a silver sword slashed across the neck of a Bloodseeker. The creature fell, revealing a dark-skinned woman swathed in an emerald green light.

I can't hold them off long. We don't have much time, don't waste it watching me, sounded her voice inside Miguel's head. Heeding her warning, and happy to see another like him, he dove beneath the surface and plowed his hand through the muddy bottom, grasping hold of a chain. Clutching it tight, he came back up to the surface. The woman was none other than the emerald Slayer and she needed his immediate help as several Bloodseekers circled her. She twisted in a circle, her sword pointed outward in one hand and a wooden stake in the other.

He swam towards the shore, the glowing agate amulet flowing behind his hand as he gripped the silver chain. His movement in the water caught the attention of the Bloodseekers' sensitive hearing and half moved towards him as the other half hissed at Emerald.

They moved at incredible speed and he was lifted off the ground. A firm grasp around his neck, before he could drop the amulet over his head. Its eyes blazed through his. *You will give me the amulet!*

Miguel's arm moved without his consent and the amulet hovered above the Bloodseeker's hand.

No stop! Divert your eyes! Emerald shouted inside his head.

Miguel squeezed his eyes shut but the power of the Bloodseeker's glare made it a battle to close them. He fought it, forcing with all his strength to shut them.

You cannot fight me!

"Yes I can!" he shouted with a burst of strength hiding inside him. If he didn't combat the Bloodseekers mind control he'd lose the amulet, and they'd be unable to fulfill their destinies. With every ounce of will, he forced his eyes shut, knocking the Bloodseeker out of his head. He wrapped the chain around his hand until the stone touched his skin.

"No!" screeched in his ears and echoed as his body was enveloped in a light so bright he saw it through shut eyes. Opening them, light blasted from his body and crossed the field of flowers. Every Bloodseeker turning to ash before his eyes and their anguish rising inside him.

They didn't choose to be what they were, but were compelled. Their souls writhed in misery, tormented for eternity.

The light vanished and Emerald stood before him, their eyes sizzling as he clutched the stone and unwound the chain from his wrist, dropping it over his head.

Chapter 1

She tucked his hair behind his ear and whispered something in it. Her lips brushed his face and rested on his lips where he returned a passionate kiss.

Opal's eyes widened. She couldn't believe Lynden was kissing another girl. Unable to drag her eyes away from the sight as she fumed. He was here with her family! *Who does he think he is?!*

She had the mind to walk up to them and kick him between the legs, but that'd only make her look like a crazed, jealous girlfriend. She took a deep breath and let it out so hard it blew her bangs from her forehead. Opal turned and leaned against the wall. Laughter from couples and families happily eating dinner drifted into her ears.

"Excuse me," said a woman as she walked past Opal. The woman wore a tight dress that showed curves people didn't need to see. Opal cringed and hoped one day she wouldn't look like her as she twisted back around and peered onto the patio. They were gone. She peered around the corner and didn't see him there either, so she scooted around the corner and negotiated the crowd as she slipped out the back.

The back door opened onto the beach and the resort was a straight shot over two miles long. She shrugged. The walk would give her time to cool down and maybe her family would be back. She shouldn't have left them to have a romantic night with Lynden, but they'd had no privacy in the suite. Her parents were always around and her little brother was up her butt all the time.

Every time she spotted a couple she halted immediately, assuming it was them, but it never was. *What a jerk! And I thought he was such a good guy!* She had a good sense of character and never saw him cheating on her. From him, she'd always felt admiration, which was the only reason she'd given him a chance. *How could he betray me?*

She seethed when she realized they had two more days at the resort. Grabbing handfuls of her strawberry blonde hair, she cringed at the idea of acting like everything was OK. *Should I tell my parents? Oh, I don't know what to do!*

The doorman greeted Opal as she entered the hotel. She painted on a smile in return. Her face didn't feel like smiling but it wasn't the doorman's fault her boyfriend was a cheating creep. *And the young woman was gorgeous!* Opal had a high opinion of herself and admired her own long legs, firm stomach, and fine facial features. Men of all ages ogled her, but *she* was flawless and even Opal admitted she had a couple unwanted scars and wished her boobs were one cup size larger. Her long platinum blonde hair hung in perfect styled waves and her skin was supple and taut. *She looked like a freakin' movie star! URR!*

She slid the key across the pad and the door unlocked. The suite was quiet, meaning no one was home, so she slipped into her room. The window was still open and a warm, salty, ocean breeze blew the curtains into the room making a rounded plume. She walked onto the empty balcony and leaned against the railing. Children giggling drifted through the air, catching her attention. This made her smile for real. A brown-haired boy no more than six splashed and kicked as a little girl, most likely his sister, splashed and kicked and they tossed a ball back and forth.

To the right was an outdoor hot tub and it was empty. This gave her an idea and she slipped her sexiest bikini on. She'd bought it earlier when she and Lynden went shopping. It was mostly strings with small breast cups that barely covered everything. Her parents would hate it and make her take it off, but what they didn't know wouldn't hurt them. Smiling, she flipped her straight hair that immediately fell back against her cheek as she admired her reflection in the mirror. Her eyes lit up and she grabbed her cell. Making pouty lips, she took a few selfies and posted them.

She lowered herself into the hot tub. The warm water bubbled around her and she put her head back, looking up to the sky. It was a clear night, not a single cloud littered the sky to block the twinkling stars. She was ready to get out when a group of teens paying no mind to her settled into the hot tub. Their pale bodies immaculate and unblemished. They dropped into the other side of the tub. She gulped as insecurity passed through like race horses, then glanced at their faces.

There were three, one a tall male, is hair shaven on the sides with a thick, raven strip in the center tied back in a ponytail. His rectangular face cleanly shaven, but his eyes made the biggest impression on Opal. They were a bright blue like an azure gemstone shining amongst a pile of conglomerate rocks. A female, the moonlight shining against her shimmery, light brown hair and eighteen carat gold eyes. Opal's own eyes were a unique shade of gold, but she considered them more a fourteen carat gold alloy. Alloy or not, her eyes defined her and grabbed the attention of others.

"The light is perfect tonight for moon-bathing," said the other female.

Opal shifted her eyes and they widened. She gasped. It was the same blonde female she'd seen Lynden with earlier. *Where is he?* she thought, her eyes dancing around the pool area. She'd last seen him with her. Panic worked its way into her gut and she decided to stay. It wasn't something she could explain or put her finger on, but she'd always had a sixth sense and right now it told her something bad had happened to him.

Message From the Author

I have lived near St. Augustine for two decades and immediately fell in love with the city. It's the oldest U.S. city, located on the Atlantic coast in North Florida. Its history is steeped in suspense and paranormal activities; ghost, pirates and more. So why not vampires?

When the idea for the series seeded itself in my mind, I found an article online about vampires in St. Augustine. After much research, I never learned if it was fact or fiction, but lean towards fiction. The seed sprouted a stem and gave me an entirely different idea.

After more research, I discovered an archaeologist at Flagler College has been digging up St. Augustine, finding buried treasure; houses, subdivisions, skeletons and much more. My idea blossomed and the prologue to The Vampires Next Door was born. The first St. Augustine Novella in the Bloodseeker series.

In honor of the history local to my home I took a different approach with The Monster Upstairs, Book Two in the Bloodseeker Series. There are tunnels beneath Jacksonville that were used for transportation and others used by bankers and still to this day used by businesses. There are even tours that take people into them. As a resident of the area, I've heard many stories about them being used during prohibition. I never discovered if that's true but did find plenty of interesting information which I used in writing this story.

The fort fight scene: I originally planned on using Castillo de San Marcos Fort but after talking with a local reader I learned about Fort Matanzas. After doing a little research, I realized how isolated it was, making it a much better spot. I wasn't able to take pictures of my own since the ferry isn't running there due to damage from Hurricane Matthew. The storm did much damage to the area and I was extremely lucky as it took a jog further off coast as it neared the county I live.

I want to thank my wonderful street team and editor for their great danger ideas while Alison is meandering through the tunnels searching for Rodham and Adrian's amulets.

Included in the book is a picture of Wolf Manor in Tennessee, taken by the author. The cover background is an actual photo of the fort bridge. I believe it is Castillo de San Marcos, but am not able to confirm that.

Sources Used:

"Hurricane Matthew: Surveying damage in St. Augustine the morning after." *St. Augustine Record.* N.p., 02 Nov. 2016. Web. 29 Jan. 2017.

Juropa08. "UnderGround Jax." *YouTube.* YouTube, 13 May 2013. Web. 29 Jan. 2017.

Soergel, Matt. "St. Augustine's City Archaeologist Sees What Lies beneath."*StAugustine.com.* The St. Augustine Record, 15 June 2015. Web. 06 Mar. 2016

"Union Station Tunnels Intact." *Union Station Tunnels Intact | Metro Jacksonville.* N.p., 14 Jan. 2008. Web. 29 Jan. 2017.

Wolf Manor Tennesee
Taken by author

Fort Matanzas

About the Author

Elle Klass is the author of mystery, suspense, and contemporary fiction. Her works include *As Snow Falls, Eye of the Storm Eilida's Tragedy*, and the *Baby Girl* series. Her work *Eye of the Storm Eilida's Tragedy* is a Reader's Favorite Fiction-Paranormal Finalist in the 2015 Reader's Favorite Awards. *Baby Girl Box Set* received Official Honors in Young Adult through New Apple Indie Ebook Awards. She is a night-owl where her imagination feeds off shadows, and creaks in the attic. Visit her website at elleklass.weebly.com